BIRTHDAY GIFT

MARY WATERFORD

To Nora Roberts
For the comfort and inspiration

PROLOGUE

*A*s the sky faded to a soft mauve and stars began to dot the horizon, William Locke heaved a sigh. The lighthouse rose behind him, the one hundred- and fifty-year-old sandstone brick tinted by the setting sun. A light breeze ruffled William's dark hair and he pushed his fingers through it, unsettled. This place was perfect. Exactly what his family wanted. They knew how these things worked, what their clients demanded. As corporate retreats went, the Blessed Inlet lighthouse and surrounding buildings would fit the bill impeccably.

The buildings themselves needed a fair bit of work; they had barely been looked after over the last fifty years. The road up from the beach might need to be widened. Parking would have to be expanded, perhaps some accommodation added. Equally distanced from both Melbourne and Sydney, it would attract clients from both. So, what was wrong with it? Or maybe more accurately, what was wrong with him? These sorts of situations usually gave him a buzz of excitement, following the thrill of success. His job in the family business was location scout and he was damned good at it and for years, had loved it. But just recently, there was that creeping sense of ennui, of dissatisfaction. Just a creeping question of "what was the point of it all?" that he couldn't shake. He rolled his shoulders and moved his head from side to side, the tight little ball of frustration in his gut was undeniable. Pushing the thoughts aside, he turned away from the cliffs and the Tasman Sea, heading around the buildings to his car. It was a six-hour drive back to Sydney and he wasn't going to get there until after midnight as it was. Best to make a move.

He drove down the steep, curving track away from the lighthouse, tooling the black Porsche Cayman through the little town of Blessed Inlet. It didn't take long, a town of just over one thousand people didn't take up much space. Turning on Inlet Road, William shifted through the gears and gunned the Porsche, heading for the highway. Tall gum trees lined the road, their pale trunks turning skeletal in the fading light.

He swore as he approached the turn off onto the Princes Highway and a truck came roaring past him, doing at least twenty kilometers over the speed limit. Maniac, he thought to himself. He pulled out onto the sorry excuse for a highway. It was less a highway and more just a ribbon of road winding through the state forest before turning North and crossing the border, heading up the East coast to Sydney.

He grinned as the road took a wide curve and he pressed on the accelerator, feeling the car hug the asphalt as it turned into the camber. As he exited the curve and straightened the wheel, something registered at the edge of his vision, but focused as he was on driving, he didn't allow it to intrude. As he continued along the highway though, it niggled at him. It could have been a car accident. The more he thought about it, the more that seemed the most likely scenario. Heaving a sigh, he waited for the next turnout in the road and circled back. Within a few minutes, he was at the site and sure enough, a car had gone off the road, tires sliding across the gravel and into the wide trunk of a mountain ash, its hazard lights flashing.

He pulled in behind, noting that there was no damage to the back or sides of the little Honda Civic, so maybe it was ok. He got out of the Porsche, grabbing his cell phone and sliding it into his pocket.

"Hello?" he called out, approaching the driver's side of the car. The door was pushed open, but the driver was nowhere in sight. The car was piled high with stuff; bags, pictures, blankets, a birdcage—but no driver. What the fuck? "Hellooo?" He called out, louder this time, peering into the gloom beyond the beam of his headlights.

"Help." A soft, female voice all but whispered, the voice tight with pain.

Grabbing his phone, William switched the torch app on and shone it towards the sound of the voice. He took a few steps forward, holding the phone high to maximize the reach of the light. Another few steps revealed a woman, leaning against the trunk of a tree, her back to him. Wild, blond curls cascaded over her shoulders and down her back. Her feet were bare.

"Shit! Are you okay?" He rushed forward as she turned. A hot, oily lump of dread curled in his stomach as he saw her. She was heavily pregnant, her arm curled protectively around her stomach. He met her eyes, pale green and filled with terror.

"Thank goddess. Please help me. I've-" she gasped, doubling over. William moved closer, reaching out a hand, not sure if he should touch her or not. After a moment that seemed to last an eternity, the pain passed, and the woman straightened. "I've

3

gone into labor. My phone's dead. The baby's not due for another three or four weeks. I don't know what to do." The rising note of panic in her voice was unmistakable.

"Alright. It's alright." He quickly punched triple zero into his phone, refusing to dwell on the knowledge that the nearest ambulance would have to be at least forty-five minutes away and that was the absolute best case scenario. "I'm calling an ambulance."

"Dispatch. Police, fire or ambulance."

"Ambulance, please."

"Where are you calling from?"

"Victoria. Ah, on the highway."

"What is your nearest town?"

"Um, probably Genoa."

"One moment while I put you through."

He waited while the call connected, painfully unsure of what to do as the woman stood by the tree, her arm still holding her bulging belly. "What's your name?"

"Juniper. What's yours?"

"William."

"Well, William, thanks for stopping. I really appreciate it."

He had to appreciate that she was making an effort to control the perfectly understandable panic that must have been gripping her.

"Ambulance Victoria. What's the emergency?" The voice was female and very professional sounding. He was oddly comforted, even though he couldn't see how a disembodied voice on the other end of a phone line could help him here, no matter how professional she sounded.

"Ah, yeah, hi. I've just stopped to give assistance at a roadside accident and there's a woman here who appears to be in labor."

As if on cue, Juniper doubled over again, giving a low moan as she did so.

"Ok, you're calling from a mobile. You need to give me as much information about your location as possible."

He quickly calculated in his head, thinking back to the last sign post he'd driven past and told her.

"Okay, can you tell me what's going on there? You said a woman has had a car accident and is in labor, correct?"

"Yes, that's correct."

"Is the woman conscious and breathing?"

"Yes, to both."

"Great. She can talk and speaks English?"

"Yes, to both again."

"Can you ascertain what injuries she has, if any?"

"Juniper, are you injured at all? Juniper?" She had pushed off from the tree and was heading away from the road, down a slight embankment, into the scrub. He followed her, feeling a stab of fear. She seemed to be in a daze. Maybe she'd hit her head? She stopped, holding onto a tree branch as she rubbed her back., "Juniper, honey, you have to talk to me. Are you injured at all?"

The urgent note in his voice got her attention and she turned and looked back at him. "No, I don't think so. My neck hurts a bit." She rubbed at her chest. "Maybe my chest, from the seat-belt, I think."

"She says she has no injuries but her neck hurts," William said into the phone.

"Ok, that's good news. What about the labor? Has her water broken?"

He checked, Juniper said no. "No."

"Can you ask her how far along she is in the pregnancy?"

He relayed the question to Juniper. "She says about thirty-six weeks."

"Any complications or contraindications?"

He followed Juniper, who seemed to be wandering aimlessly through the bush. He didn't think it was a good idea to get too far away from the road, but he couldn't see how he could stop her, short of manhandling her, which he definitely wasn't prepared to do. "Juniper, the dispatcher wants to know if you've had any complications or anything?"

She shook her head, her back still to him as she walked.

"She says no."

"A truck ran me off the road." She'd stopped in a small clearing, turning and looking up at the sky as she spoke. William followed her gaze. The moon was rising, just floating on the edge of the horizon, bright white against the night sky. "He came around the bend, halfway over on my side of the road. I swerved, hit the gravel, then hit the tree. But I'd been having contractions, on and off all day. Just thought they were Braxton Hicks."

He relayed all of that information to the woman on the other end of the line.

"Right, I've sent an ambulance, but they're going to be a while. The nearest available station is Blessed Inlet, so you're looking at forty-five to fifty minutes. Can you tell me how far apart her contractions are?"

His worst fears realized; William forced himself to stay calm as he tried to figure it out. From when he'd first stopped to standing in the clearing, she'd had two contractions. "Maybe four or five minutes."

He could hear her typing on the other end of the line. "Ok, I'm going to stay on the line with you until the ambulance arrives. If you like, put me on speaker and put the phone down. You might need both hands."

William swallowed convulsively as he hoped desperately that she didn't mean he might need two hands to deliver the baby. He put the phone on speaker and put it in the top pocket of his shirt, thanking the heavens that it was fully charged. "Okay, Juniper, the ambulance is going to be a while, so it's just you and me for now."

She nodded, both hands cupping her bump as she gazed at the moon and swayed gently, back and forth. The silvery light of the moon caressed her face and toyed with the riotous curls falling over her shoulders. His breath caught in his throat. She looked so beautiful, like an earth mother. Then her face scrunched up in pain and he stepped forward, instinctively putting his arms around her before her knees gave way. She brought her hands up to his shoulders, gripping on tight. As the contraction passed, she rested her forehead on his chest and her grip eased. "I'm so scared."

William rubbed both hands up and down her back, desperately wishing he could give her some genuine comfort. "I won't let anything happen to you, okay?" Well, if that wasn't the most ridiculous thing he could have said. They were out in the bush, miles from any meaningful assistance and she was in full blown labor. It was difficult to imagine a worse situation. She raised her head and looked at him for a long moment. Her pale green eyes were luminous in the moonlight, and he felt like she was seeing straight through to his very soul.

"Okay." He felt a surge of surprise, but then she smiled at him. She knew damn well he was offering her cold comfort. He smiled back. "Talk to me. Distract me," she said.

"Right, okay." He racked his brains. What did you talk about with a woman you didn't know, who was having a baby in the bush, to distract her from said baby? He couldn't think of a single goddamn thing, so he went with, "Where were you driving to, tonight?"

"I was going to stop overnight in Eden. I'm heading to Byron Bay, to visit my grandmother. She's going to help me have a water birth..." Her voice trailed off as she realized that was no longer an option. She sighed. "Maybe I should have stayed in Melbourne."

"You're from Melbourne?"

"Yes, born and bred. But there's nothing there for me now."

He wanted to ask about the baby's father but there was such sadness in her voice that he didn't think it appropriate. She didn't have parents? Siblings?

She turned in his arms, resting her head on his shoulder and sighed. "Is this okay?"

"Yeah, sure." He wasn't sure what to do with his hands now that she was facing away but she solved that problem by taking them in hers and resting them on her belly. Well, now it was getting weird. Weird, but...nice. He'd never touched a pregnant belly before. It was really quite amazing, to think that a tiny human was in there and soon it would be out. Okay, it might be best not to give that too much thought. He felt her belly tighten, harden as she gasped, gripping his hands tight. He gripped back, giving her something to hold on to.

When the contraction was over, she said, "Is it too weird if I ask you to rub my belly?"

Ah yes, a bit. "No, it's fine." He moved his hands gently over her bump. It really was miraculous. She started swaying again and he moved with her. Honestly, whatever she needed, she was going to get at this point.

"I like the moon. It makes me feel calm."

He glanced up. The moon was peaking above the treetops now, spilling into the clearing. A bright white halo had formed around it. It looked amazing.

"It's a special one tonight. Maybe it's a sign, a good night to have a baby."

"I'm sure it is." Not that he ever went for that sort of thing, but she seemed totally the type and again, whatever she needed to get her through, she was going to get.

The moment dragged out, just gentle belly rubs and slow swaying. It was mesmerizing, until another contraction hit. Once it passed, she resumed swaying, so he resumed the belly rubs. She was quiet, taking deep, controlled breaths and gazing at the moon. A few more contractions came and went but then the next one was really bad. It seemed to drag on longer than the others and William felt another stab of fear.

"Fuck, that hurt."

"Sir?"

He jolted. He had completely forgotten about the lady on the phone, in his pocket.

"Yes?"

"The ambulance is about twelve minutes away. Everything okay there?"

"I don't know. The contractions seem worse."

"They are coming a bit faster now, about three minutes apart. Hold tight, help's not far away."

"Thanks."

He was grateful that someone was across the situation enough to time them; he'd seen enough movies to know that was probably important. He felt Juniper take a deep breath, then another. He'd seen that in movies too, it seemed like the right thing to do. Maybe this was all going to be okay. It wasn't long before another contraction hit her and it was definitely worse than the previous ones, lasting longer and leaving her breathless.

"What do you need?" He asked when it had passed.

"I don't know. Maybe some drugs." She laughed breathlessly when she realized how that must have sounded. "You know, like the happy gas or something."

"You can't imagine how much I wish I could give you that right now." That was the honest truth.

She laughed again. "Unfortunately, it's not the sentiment that counts in this situation."

"Fair enough."

"I think I need to sit down."

"Okay." William tightened his grip on her as her knees seemed to give way and carefully lowered her to the ground, narrowly avoiding a large tree root curling out of the ground. With nowhere else for him to go, he sat behind her, putting a leg on either side of her hips. "Is this okay?"

"Yes, this is good."

She rested her head back on his shoulder, drawing in more deep, steadying breaths. Then he heard her breath catch and braced himself for another contraction.

"I hope the baby's okay." She said it so softly he almost didn't hear her, then he realized she was crying and his heart almost broke. She was doing an amazing job of covering up her fear, but this really was the worst situation to be having a baby in. Too many weeks early, miles from proper medical care.

"It will be." He cursed himself for how vapid the words sounded, even to his own ears. She was saved from replying by another contraction. He winced as she laid a hand on each of his thighs and gripped very tightly. The moan she gave was so animalistic and agonized that it chilled him to the bone.

The voice in his pocket spoke up again. "Two minutes. You'll be able to hear the sirens soon."

"Tell them we're off the road, down an embankment, in a clearing. Maybe fifty meters off the road."

"Will do."

At that moment, he heard the faint, distant wail of the ambulance sirens. Thank fuck. He had never felt such a feeling of blessed relief in his entire life. "Can you hear that, Juniper? The ambulance is nearly here."

Another contraction ripped through her. He took her hands to stop the death grip on his thighs as she turned her face into his neck and moaned. It seemed to go on forever. The sirens drew closer, closer, closer. Then he could see the lights flashing through the trees, hear the crunch of the tires on the gravel at the roadside. The lady on the phone let them know she was going to sign off and wished them luck as William heard a female voice call out.

"Helloooo? Where are you guys?" A bright light swung through the trees as one of the paramedics waved a torch around.

"Back here!" William took his phone out, switched the torch app on and waved it high above his head.

"Okay! We've got you."

He heard two sets of boots crash through the scrub then the sweetest sight that ever met his eyes emerged into the clearing. Two medical professionals, kitted out in all sorts of medical gear, looking very capable. Maybe there was a god.

"Okay, let's see what we've got here." The female paramedic walked over and knelt down in front of them, placing a molded plastic kit and a red canvas bag on the ground next to her. "I'm Mikky. This is my partner Rafe." The male paramedic crouched down and gave them both a reassuring smile, his dark eyes gleaming in the moonlight.

"I'm William, this is Juniper."

"Nice to meetcha. Mind if I take a look?" Mikky had taken a pair of rubber gloves out of the kit and wriggled her fingers into them in under two seconds. Juniper shook her head. She lifted the hem of Juniper's dress. "Right, we're going to have to get your underwear off. Lift your hips if you can, honey." William braced to enable Juniper to push against him and lift her hips as Mikky quickly removed her underwear. The moon gleamed on her red hair as she bent forward. "Okay, you're fully dilated. I think we need to get you to the ambulance right now."

"No...no, please no." The anxiety in Juniper's voice was palpable but any response was forestalled by another contraction.

William saw Rafe and Mikky exchange a look, then Rafe calmly rose and strode off across the clearing and back through the scrub.

"I think we've got no choice anyway, love. Rafe's gone to get us a few things to help us along. What can we do to make you more comfortable?"

"I don't know."

"Do you think you're okay as you are? Or do you want to lie down, stand up, get on all fours?"

"I think I'm okay here."

Mikky met William's gaze. "You good with that?"

"Sure."

"Good man."

Mikky opened the red bag and pulled out a whistle, offering it to Juniper. "Use this for the next contraction, if you want to. It's methoxyflurane. It'll help with the pain."

"Drugs. Thank fuck," Juniper said, taking it gratefully.

Rafe returned with some plastic sheeting, towels, blankets, a water bottle. He twisted the cap off and handed it to Juniper. She drank deeply, dropping the bottle and crying out before she remembered the whistle and sucked on it desperately. The contraction seemed to last forever and even to William's inexperienced eye, things were ramping up. Rafe and Mikky moved swiftly, in perfect unison. "Not long now, Juniper. We're going to set you up as best we can. Rafe is gonna lift you up a little while William and I slide this sheet under you, okay?" At Juniper's nod, Rafe slid an arm under her knees while William put his hands under her arms. Mikky counted down, three, two, one and in no time at all, Juniper was leaning back against him again, the sheeting and some towels under her. It was just in time as another contraction hit and she drew on the whistle. It was something, at least.

When it finally passed, she was sobbing, "I don't want to do this. I don't want to do this."

Mikky, kneeling between Juniper's feet, grinned at her cheekily, "Bit late for that now, love."

Juniper laughed and sobbed at the same time. "True." She took a deep breath, in through her nose and out through her mouth. "What sort of name's Mikky, anyway?"

Mikky laughed. "Short for Mikayla."

"Gotta love that. Trash talking in the middle of labor," Rafe said with a chuckle.

"That's it! You're a trooper, Juniper. You've got this. On the next contraction, if you feel you want to push, go for it."

William felt the intensity of the next contraction in his gut as Juniper pushed back hard against him, holding his hand in a knuckle crunching grip. She made an otherworldly keening sound, forgetting about the whistle in her other hand. When it passed, she said, "I want to push, but I can't." She moved her legs restlessly, looking for purchase.

Mikky shot Rafe a look and he shifted forward, taking her bare-foot in his hand. He placed it against his hip, rubbing the top. "I've got you, darling. Brace against me."

"And here." Mikky settled Juniper's foot against the tree root just near her. "See how you go on the next push, if you're not comfy, we'll figure something out."

"Okay. It's coming again, I can feel it. Oh god, I can't. I can't."

"Look at the moon. Just look at the moon." William cursed himself as soon as the words were out.

"The moon! Why the fuck would I want to look at the fucking moon! The moon's not going to come down here and get this fucking baby out of meeeee....aahhhhhh!"

"Fair point," William said.

She bore down hard, straining, pushing her chin down on her chest and groaning, long and loud. "What was that?"

"That was your water breaking, it's all good." Rafe handed Mikky some towels and she quickly laid them on the plastic sheeting.

On another contraction, Mikky said, "That's it, Juniper, amazing. Not long to go, I promise."

There was a short respite before another contraction hit, more pushing, more screaming, then a pause, then Juniper did it all again.

"This is it, love. I can see the baby's head. Let's go."

On the next contraction, Mikky pushed Juniper's dress high on her hips to get it out of the way and William could see the baby's head emerging. He took a deep breath as he felt the blood drain from his face. This was a really big deal. An actual baby... coming out of her.

"You right there, William?" Rafe asked.

"Me? Yeah, of course." Get your shit together, man, you're not the one having the baby, he said to himself.

"One more big push, honey, and your baby will be here."

On the next push, Mikky adeptly caught the baby as it slithered out. In one smooth move, she held the baby up. William thought it was simultaneously the ugliest and most beautiful sight he'd ever seen. All purple, covered in gunk, it looked like an alien. Its face was all crumpled, like a miniature Winston Churchill. Juniper reached for it and Mikky grinned widely as she passed the baby into her arms. "You've got yourself a little boy." Rafe tucked a space blanket around them both, and William shifted so his arms were outside the blanket, and he could still hold her.

Juniper cradled the baby against her chest and leaned back on William as the baby let out a loud, lusty wail. Her chest was heaving with the effort and she sobbed, "I did it...I did it."

William stroked her hair back from her forehead. "You sure did." She turned her face against his neck, and he cradled her as she cradled her baby.

The paramedics gave her a little time to get her breath before Rafe said, "I think we should get you moving, darling."

"Right, okay." Juniper was still breathless.

Mikky took a clamp and scissors from the kit. "We'll do this first or things are gonna get real awkward, real fast." She looked at Juniper, reading something in her face. "William, to do the honors?"

At Juniper's nod, she offered the scissors to William. He took the scissors with a shaking hand. It felt like a significant moment, something the baby's father should do. He felt honored that Juniper had asked him to do it. He reached down between Juniper's legs and as he cut the cord, made a wish for the baby, that he would have a full and happy life. When he handed the scissors back, Rafe turned to Mikky, "How do you think we should do this?"

"I'll take the baby, you take everything else, William can help Juniper. Sound like a plan?" As they all nodded, she rose to her feet and bent to take the squalling baby in her arms, tucking a blanket around him firmly. Rafe helped Juniper up and wrapped the sterile sheeting around her waist, then the space blanket.

~

illiam stood, rolling his shoulders and flexing his hands. Now that it was over, he hadn't realized how much of a workout that had been. He reached for Juniper as Rafe let her go and she stumbled a little.

"Sorry, my legs are a little shaky."

"No problem."

"You got her?" Rafe hefted the kit, the bags and the torch.

"Yep." Rather than make her walk, William swung her up in his arms, smiling when she gasped in surprise. "I've got you." He looked down at her for a long moment, caught. "You trust me?"

"Yes." She sighed, wrapping her arms around his neck and letting her head fall on his shoulder. He moved forward, following Rafe as he held the light high, leading them out of the clearing. Climbing the embankment was the hardest part and he had to stifle a groan, feeling more than a tinge of relief when Rafe pulled the gurney out of the back of the ambulance, and he was able to lay Juniper carefully down. Mikayla handed the baby over and William stood, looking down at both of them. Juniper met his gaze.

"I'm not sure what to say. I don't have the words to acknowledge what you just did for me."

He felt deeply moved. "You don't have to say anything."

She reached up and caressed his cheek. "Thank you."

"I'm not going to say any time, because, you know, let's not do that again." He smiled as she laughed. Without giving it a second thought, he leaned down and pressed a kiss on her forehead, then ran a finger along the baby's cheek. "You're welcome," he said, looking at her, again caught in that sea green gaze. Then he stepped back to allow Rafe and Mikky to take over, sliding the gurney into the ambulance, Mikky stepping in behind. She turned to pull the door shut, giving William a smile and a wave. He looked at Juniper one more time as she held the baby close and dropped her head back on the pillow, her eyes closed and a sweet smile curving her lips.

"Great job, mate. I don't know what would have happened to her if you hadn't stopped."

The two men shook hands. "Cheers," William said. Then Rafe was in behind the wheel, starting the engine, pulling onto the road. He gave the horn a toot as he pulled away and in seconds, he was around the bend and out of sight. William stood on the side of the road in the dark for a long moment, feeling oddly bereft. Christ, what an experience. He reached for his phone, thinking to call his sister to tell her all about it. His heart skipped a beat when he saw he had twelve missed calls from her and two text messages, imploring him to call her, urgently.

"Cassie, what is it?"

"Jesus, William. Where the fuck have you been? It's Dad. We think he's had a stroke."

"What? How?"

"Please come. I'm so scared. He's gone in an ambulance, Mum's with him. I'm on my way to the hospital but I don't want to be there alone if —" Her voice broke on a sob.

"Okay, I'm on my way, but I'm hours away. Which hospital?" She rattled off the details as he got in the car, his hands shaking as he pushed the key in the ignition and turned it. He swore gratefully when it started. He'd left the headlights on that whole time. "I'm on my way." He hung up and gunned the engine, pulling out onto the highway, the gravel skittering under his tires.

CHAPTER 1

*A*lmost three years later

"*Y*eah, Cass. It'll be great." William, his cell phone in one hand, typed away at his laptop keyboard with the other. "Like we always said, it's going to be a real point of difference. Not many companies can offer a real, bona fide lighthouse for a corporate retreat."

"Yeah, exactly. I'll send you the projections for the first twelve months after we go live. I've already scouted out some of our existing clients and they're very keen to book, so I'm not going to go too conservative on the figures. You just get me the estimated date to work from."

"Okay. I'm meeting with the builder in about ten minutes. But just a heads up, it's a lot of work, probably our biggest project yet, so it's gonna take a while."

"Oh, poor you, stuck in a pretty seaside town for weeks on end. My heart bleeds for you."

"Haha, funny. It is pretty nice though."

"Maybe you could invite what's her name down to hang out, if you get bored."

"Her name's Sharon and ah, no, I won't be doing that."

Cassie sighed. "Like that, is it? And we didn't even get the chance to meet her. Not that we ever do."

"You're seriously getting into this with me now?"

Another sigh. "No, sorry. It's just that Mum and I are a bit worried about you." She paused. "I swear I just heard your eyes roll."

"Probably, because they did." He smiled when he heard her chuckle.

"Okay, well, I'll let you go, but before I do that, I'm gonna let you know something."

"What?" He asked with trepidation.

"I'm going to talk my future father-in-law into producing a new reality tv show. It'll be called *The Businessman Wants a Wife.* I'll give you one guess who the businessman will be."

"Thanks, but no thanks. I don't want a wife. And he's not your future father-in-law until James pops the question."

"Sure you do. And it's just a matter of time before James pops the question. He's not a laggard, like some people I know. Now I'm going to hang up before your eyes roll all the way to the back of your head. Bye!"

William shook his head as he threw his cellphone down on the foldout table he'd set up on the terrace at the back of the small cottage. It offered a spectacular view of the sea. He'd only been there a few days, but he'd already started to enjoy the ever-changing view offered by the ocean vista. Today it was a hard, iron gray under a restless sky. He didn't think it was overstating things to say that it matched his mood perfectly. As much as he thought his sister had been wrong about most of what she'd said on the phone, she was right about one thing; stuck in a pretty seaside town was not the worst place to be right now. Being in Sydney with the work demands, the social life, the bar hopping, the dating, it all just seemed so meaningless. So empty. He heard the sound of a truck trundling up the steep track and gave himself a mental shake. Time to put his game face on.

~

*W*illiam stood on the beach in Blessed Inlet, the warm sand between his toes, the hot breeze ruffling his hair. The sky was a clear, cloudless blue with a summer brightness that almost hurt the eyes. The ocean was calm, the waves washing in gently to the shore before pulling out, the endless pattern somewhat mesmerizing. It had been a long three years since he had last been in town. So much had happened. His father's stroke, although not lethal, had left him a shell of his former self, unable to fulfill his commitments to the family business. His mother, ever the devoted wife, had also stepped back from the business as much as she could, to look after her husband. It was endless rounds of physiotherapy, osteopathy, speech pathology, pretty much anything the medical team and William's mother could come up with. He was in much better condition than his doctors had originally advised. His dad could walk now, with the aid of a frame, and his speech was only slightly slurred. But he tired easily and sometimes found it hard to stay focused. Consequently, William's role in the business had changed, practically overnight. He'd stepped up, of course. He loved his family and would do anything for them. But that creeping ennui he'd begun feeling a few years back, had grown into a gnawing restlessness that churned in his gut. He felt caged but confused because even if he managed to break out of the cage, he had no idea where he would want to go. He heaved a sigh, turning to walk along the waterline, oblivious to the waves swirling around his ankles, wetting the bottom of his slacks.

He thought about the last time he'd been in Blessed Inlet and of the woman, Juniper. What an experience that had been. He wondered about her sometimes, hoped that she'd made it to her grandmother in Byron Bay.

"William!" The warning tone was unmistakable and had him confused.

He looked up to see a woman running towards the ocean, honey-colored legs flashing under a blue skirt, blonde curls streaming behind her. She was chasing a small child, who shrieked with laughter as she scooped him up and spun him around. "I said stay away from the water! We'll go swimming in a little while." She put him back on his feet and glanced up, catching William staring at her. As their eyes met, William felt the breath leave his lungs in a whoosh. It was Juniper. Here. In Blessed Inlet. She looked at him uncertainly for a long moment. He must have looked like an absolute psychopath, standing on the beach just staring at her. He watched as comprehension dawned and uncertainty turned to recognition. She bent and said something to the boy, giving him a nudge and watching for a moment as he headed to a picnic blanket further up the beach. Then she turned to William again and smiled. Christ. She was absolutely stunning. She moved towards him, and the beach faded away, the sounds, the smells, the heat. It was just her. The sun gilding her hair a bright gold, her pale green eyes never leaving his. She looked like a woodland nymph, wild and earthy. Then she was there, in front of him, stepping closer, winding her arms around his neck. Of their own volition, his arms went around her, pulling her close. He held her for the longest time and felt, for just a moment, that ever-present churning in his gut eased. She pulled back and looked up at him.

"I didn't think I'd ever see you again."

"Me either. I thought you were going to Byron Bay."

"Well, plans change." She laughed and took his hand in hers. "Come and meet your namesake."

He tightened his grip on her fingers. "You named your baby after me?"

"I did. Of course, I did." She gave him a dazzling smile. "We call him Billy, but his full name is William Archer Bell."

"Juniper, I…"

She tilted her head to one side, looking up at him doubtfully. "You don't like it?"

"No, it's not that. It's just…wow." He felt a lump form in his throat and swallowed hard. "It's amazing."

She smiled in relief. "Will you come and meet him?"

"I'd love to." He followed as she led the way to the picnic blanket laid out under a beach tent, where the toddler was sitting, munching on some watermelon. The two adults with him got to their feet and he felt another start of recognition. Mikky and Rafe.

"William!" Mikky threw her arms around his neck and squeezed tight. "Amazing! Fancy seeing you here." She moved aside as Rafe stepped forward.

"Hey, mate." Rafe extended a hand and shook William's enthusiastically.

"Hi."

"Billy, come here baby." The toddler, who had been watching the exchange from behind Mikky's leg, came over to his mother, who picked him up. "This is William." The boy gazed at him for a long, unnerving moment. He had blonde curls like his mother, but where her eyes were green, his were a bright, soulful blue. He looked like he'd just stepped out of a painting of cherubs.

Juniper watched as William reached out and ran a finger down her baby's cheek, ever so gently, and her heart overflowed. Moments like this were the stuff of life. To be able to stand here, on this beach, and see this man again, it was really something. She still didn't have the words to express to him how much it meant to her that he had stayed with her that night, and how grateful she was that he had taken such good care of her. She refused to dwell on what might have happened if he hadn't doubled back after zooming past the site of her accident, but every now and then, it grabbed her, that feeling of dread; of what would have become of her and Billy if he'd kept on driving. Now, to be here, on this bright sunny day, introducing him to her son, her cup was overflowing.

"Would you like a drink?" She gestured to the picnic rug where a fold out table was laid out with chips, crackers, dips, fruit and nestled in the icebox were cans of soft drink.

"Sure. That'd be great."

They all settled around the low table as an awkward silence fell. Mikayla broke it immediately by calling it out. "Well, this is a bit awkward, hey." A laugh rippled through the group. "So, tell us, William, what the hell are you doing in Blessed Inlet?"

Juniper handed him a can of Coke, her breath hitching a little as he smiled his thanks. He was hot, to put it simply. Dark, silky hair that gleamed in the sun like sable. Warm brown eyes, long lashes. A good straight nose, full lips that made her think of kissing. She toyed with that idea for a moment. Hmm, yes, she imagined that kissing him would be quite lovely. He wasn't dressed for the beach, she thought, as she eyed his expensive business shirt and suit pants. He'd taken his shoes off, at least, as he'd walked along the sand.

"I, ah, I've got business in the area."

"For real? What kind of business? There's pretty much only caravan parks and water equipment rentals around here and I gotta say, that doesn't really look like your jam."

Bless Mikayla and her unashamedly inappropriate questions.

"It's a family business. It was actually why I was here three years ago, but then my father got sick, so we had to leave it for the moment. He's as good as he's going to get, so I'm back to pick up where I left off."

"Oh, no, what happened to your dad?"

"Stroke."

"Jeez, that's the pits. But he's better now?"

"He has a walking frame and he doesn't have much movement through his right side, among other things. But yeah, he's okay. Enough to still boss us all around, I guess." A shadow passed over his face and Juniper knew instantly that there was much more to the story than he was letting on.

"So, what's this family business then?"

"Hotels."

"Hotels? You're gonna open a hotel in Blessed Inlet?" There was no mistaking the note of skepticism in Mikayla's voice.

"Sort of."

Although it seemed that William was trying to evade her questions, Mikayla was relentless. "Come on, spill. We're not strangers here."

There was just no resisting her and William seemed to realize that fact. "Okay. My family own the lighthouse. We're looking to turn it into a corporate retreat. I'm here to organize the repairs and maintenance to get it up to scratch."

His words were met with a long, drawn-out silence that was more than uncomfortable. Rumors of the lighthouse being up for sale had been floating around a few years back. The question of who had bought it and what they planned to do with it had been the main topic of town gossip when Juniper had moved in. But then nothing had happened, for years. Now they knew why. William owned it and the only reason nothing had been done up there was because of his father falling ill. She knew her friends were wondering the same thing she was. Blessed Inlet was a small tourist town. The population hovered comfortably around one thousand residents, except in summer, when the foreshore exploded with tents and caravans, and every holiday unit was full. Except for the few weeks of crazy summer tourism, it was an artist's town, and she just couldn't see the type of accommodation he was talking about working here. Her heart sank as she pondered the types of people a corporate retreat would bring to the town. They would be the type of people she'd fled Melbourne to get away from and they were the reason she couldn't go back.

He'd started talking again, obviously aware that his revelation had caused a bit of discomfort. He was in full on business mode, selling them on the benefits, smoothly rebutting Mikayla when she objected to any changes being made at the lighthouse. It was that or let it decay and fall to ruin. Although Juniper recognized the truth of his words, she couldn't deny a twinge of disappointment. Her memories of him were obviously clouded by the conditions under which they had met, but her impression had always been one of strength and kindness, like she could trust him. Here he just seemed slick, superficial.

"What about you, Juniper? How did you end up here?" He'd turned to look at her and she couldn't avoid noticing the flare of interest in his eyes.

To give herself a bit of time, she turned to Billy, placing some more watermelon on his plate and running a hand over his bright curls. "Well, after they dropped me at the hospital, Rafe and Mikayla arranged to have my car towed back here. The mechanic said it was a write off, so Mikayla knew straight away I had no way of getting to Byron Bay. She invited me to stay at her parents for a little while, in their little cottage in their back yard." She looked at Mikayla with an affectionate grin. "It wasn't much of an invitation, actually. She'd already taken everything from my car and put it in the cottage, as well as rounding up a whole lot of secondhand baby gear to get me started." She reached over and rubbed Mikayla's arm, still so grateful for that helping hand at one of her most vulnerable moments. "A little while turned into a long while and here I am."

"Amazing. What do you do for work?"

"I own a ceramics shop, Junebug's Pots, on the main street and I run pottery classes."

"Sounds great."

"Yeah, it keeps me busy, and it gives me plenty of time to spend with Billy." She glanced at her son, who seemed to be following the exchange avidly, while managing to squash three grapes into his mouth at once. She couldn't help but smile. "We do okay, don't we, mate?" Billy grinned around the grapes and nodded his head vigorously, reaching for more fruit. "Finish what's in your mouth, first." But he didn't pull back, simply gave her a grumpy frown and extended his pudgy hand over the grapes. "William." The motherly note of warning forestalled him, and he pulled back, looking at her inquiringly. "I said, finish what's in your mouth first." Then she turned to William and found him watching her, his head tilted to one side and a smile dancing in his eyes.

"That's the exact tone my mother uses when I get in trouble."

Juniper laughed. "It's universal, encoded in our DNA during labor."

"Rafe, I wanna make a castle."

"Sure, buddy, finish your fruit and grab your hat."

As Rafe and Mikayla gathered plastic buckets and spades, Juniper slathered Billy with sunscreen and tied his sunhat on. Then they were gone, Rafe chasing a shrieking Billy to the shoreline and Mikayla bringing up the rear with the beach toys.

Juniper, smiling as she watched them go, felt William's gaze on her and turned to look at him. He was studying her with an arrested expression on his face.

"What is it?"

He shook himself. "Nothing. Sorry." A long pause followed, just drifting into awkwardness before he said, "You seem to have really landed on your feet here."

She turned to look at her friends and child, frolicking in the sand, their laughter floating on the light breeze. "I sure did."

"I'm happy for you."

She turned back to him and saw the sincerity of his words. "Thank you." Another pause. "What about you, William?"

He shrugged. "I'm good." Something about the way he said it made her want to probe, but really, she hardly knew him, and she certainly didn't have Mikayla's lack of filter for these sorts of situations. "I'd better get back." He rose to his feet and stood for a long moment looking down at her, his expression shuttered. "Seeya."

"Seeya."

Then he was gone, striding off down the beach without looking back.

~

"*Y*ou should fuck him."

"Mikayla!"

"What? You should. He definitely wants to bang you. Plus, he's hot. Way hotter than I remember him being, actually."

He was definitely hot and there was definitely something about him that pulled at Juniper. But there was also something that repelled her; that smooth operator vibe that she just didn't go for. She had been there, done that, and had no intention of going back for more. Juniper walked around the large work-bench, placing plain ceramic bowls at each stool. "Tie your hair back if you want to join the class," was all she said by way of reply.

"Okay, Mum." With a cheeky grin, her soft brown eyes twin-kling, Mikayla pulled a tie out of her pocket and piled her long, auburn hair into a messy top knot. "Better?"

"You'll do. Can you throw together the snack plate?" She went to the fridge and grabbed a chilled bottle of Sauvignon Blanc and some wine glasses from the shelf next to the fridge.

"Sure. Don't think you can distract me though."

Juniper sighed, but was saved by the buzzer at the front door to the shop. "Grab that, will you?" she said, taking over the assembly of the food platter.

"Sure."

Placing the wine and snacks in the middle of the workbench, Juniper moved to the back door, calling out to Billy. "Baby, I'm gonna start the class now if you want to come in." He immedi-ately jumped off the swing and ran towards her. Her heart swelled, as it always did in these little moments. She swept him up as he reached her. "What are you going to paint today?" She asked, moving inside and settling him at a stool.

"A turtle. It can play with Mr. Frog."

"Great idea. Here you go." She went to the shelf that lined the back wall of her small workroom and grabbed a pottery turtle she'd premade and placed it on the workbench in front of him. With the speed only a mother of toddlers possesses, she whipped his smock off the hook near the bench and jammed it over his head before he had a chance to reach for the paints. She glanced up as Mikayla came back through the beaded curtain that covered the archway, smiling at the woman who followed her. "Hi. You must be Leah."

She was short, no more than five foot three, slim with brunette hair tied back in a low ponytail and soft grey/green eyes. She smiled uncertainly. "Yes. You must be Juniper."

"That's me. Thanks for coming. Have a seat." She smiled encouragingly.

"You can sit with me," Billy piped up.

Leah smiled. "Sure, that'd be great."

Juniper handed her an apron, "Pop this on, you don't want to get paint on your lovely dress. We're using acrylics, which are very hard to get out of clothes." Juniper waited for Leah to sit down on the stool next to Billy, before continuing. "Okay, it's only you two today, so we'll get started. Just to clarify, we're painting pottery today, not making it. Have you done this before, Leah?"

"A little, but I'll probably be really bad at it."

"Don't stress. You couldn't be worse than Mikayla."

Mikayla grinned at the jibe as she removed the lids from her paint pots. "She's not wrong. No matter how much I practice, it's like I've got two thumbs when it comes to art."

"Um, most people have two thumbs?"

Juniper had to laugh at the uncertainty in Leah's voice as Mikayla cracked up laughing. "I meant all thumbs! Although hang on, would that work in my favor?"

Leah laughed. "Maybe. I don't know."

"I've got two thumbs!" Billy piped up, showing them both to Leah.

"Hey, me too," she replied, giving him the two thumbs up sign back, much to his delight.

"Mummy, can we paint now?"

"Yeah, let's go. Billy, just open one paint pot at a time. Leah and Mikayla, as long as I can trust you to mix your colors on your palette without turning everything brown, you can go ahead." She focused her attention on Leah as they both got started, knowing that Mikayla was going to be a disaster no matter how much guidance Juniper gave her. She was pretty much there for the company, wine and snacks and never pretended otherwise.

Leah carefully squirted the different colors on her palette.

"That's it. We're going to paint flowers, starting with the leaves. You want to mix your two greens like this, then take your flat brush and press out one half of the leaf. Yep, exactly like that. Now do the other half. Perfect. You're going to keep doing that, strategically around the plate, then when you think you've done enough, we'll start on the flowers."

"This is not good."

Juniper glanced over at Mikayla's first few leaves. "Maybe just have some wine." She poured out a glass and slid it across the table. "What about you, Leah? Wine or juice? I might have some soft drink in the other fridge if you'd prefer."

"Wine would be lovely, thanks."

Juniper poured the drinks, getting a juice for Billy before turning her attention back to Leah's plate. She had a sure and steady hand, laying out each leaf with precision.

"You've done this before!" Mikayla exclaimed.

Leah straightened, assessing her work. "I used to paint a lot in high school, but honestly, I haven't picked up a brush in more than ten years."

"Well, I think you've missed your calling. She's good, isn't she, Juniper?"

"Yes, she is. Here, try a flower now."

With no guidance, Leah mixed some blue and red paint to make a lovely, lush purple and laid out the flowers around the leaves.

"Purple's my favorite color!"

Leah grinned at Billy. "Mine too! Do you want some purple for your turtle?"

"Yes please!"

"So where are you staying while you're in town, Leah?" Mikayla asked, grabbing a cracker from the platter, and slathering it liberally with hummus.

"I've got a house up on Henderson's Road."

"Henderson's Road? There aren't any holiday homes up that way. The only house up there is Mr. Hend—. Wait, you don't mean Mr. Henderson's old shack? Don't tell me someone's bought that dump and is renting it out?"

"Someone has bought it, but it's not being rented out."

There was a long, confused silence before Mikayla spoke again. "You've bought it?"

Leah bent her head over her painting, looking a little self-conscious. "Yes," she said softly.

"Oh. Oh, ah, I'm so sorry. It's just that you don't look the type."

Leah frowned, perplexed. "What do you mean?"

"Well, I mean this in the best possible way. You are quite fancy, and that shack is a dump. Henderson's been trying to sell it for the better part of a decade, and it hasn't had as much as a lick of paint in all that time."

"Oh, right. Well, thank you, I guess. It's definitely a renovator's delight."

Mikayla snorted. "Renovator's delight, my ar—"

"How are you going with those flowers, Leah?" Juniper hastily interrupted, sliding a warning glance towards Billy as she cut off Mikayla's impending swear word.

"Okay, I think." She put her brush down and reached for the wine. "You really think I'm fancy?" She asked, turning to Mikayla.

"Sure, you are. That gorgeous dress you're wearing probably cost more than every dress I own, combined."

Leah hesitated, seeming to wrestle with herself for a long moment. "I'm recently divorced. My husband...ex-husband, is a wealthy real estate developer. Nine years of marriage left me with an amazing wardrobe, an old bomb of a car and just enough money to buy Henderson's shack. Honestly, I'm not that fancy, but I do love clothes."

"That sucks. The husband bit I mean, not the clothes," Mikayla said with a frown.

"It sure does. But I'll be okay. I'm planning to do up the shack. I've got a bit of experience with that sort of thing, although I've never done it on a shoestring budget, but it'll be fun."

"Good on you!" Mikayla reached across and rubbed her hand on Leah's shoulder.

"Thanks."

Mikayla grabbed her wineglass and raising it in the air, grinned at them both. "Come on girls, a toast. You too, Billy." Billy reached for his juice cup and held it high. "To Leah!"

"To Leah!"

"Oh, wow, thanks." Leah smiled shyly before taking a sip of wine.

At that moment, the front door buzzed again. "I've got to go get that. Leah, keep going with those flowers. Mikayla...have a snack."

"Right you are," Mikayla responded, reaching for the cheese knife. "Cracker, Leah?"

"Sure, thanks."

Juniper pushed the beaded curtain aside and stepped into the shop.

"William! Hi!"

"Hi."

His presence seemed to suck up all the air in the room, leaving her breathless. "I, ah..."

"This is a great shop you've got here."

"Oh, ah, thanks." She couldn't seem to gather her scattered wits enough to form a coherent sentence.

"I'm wondering if you can help me. I'm looking for a gift."

"A gift?"

"Yes, for my mother."

"Your mother?"

"Yes."

"Oh, right. Okay." She moved behind the counter, hoping to put some space between them, to calm her suddenly frazzled nerves. She felt warm all over, and her heart was stuttering uncomfortably.

He smiled at her, causing the stutter to turn into a heavy beat. His warm brown eyes surveyed her, with a glint of amusement lurking there. "You okay?"

"Me? Yeah, sure. Of course." She was not okay. He was too gorgeous for words and he was taking up a lot of space in her small shop. "You're welcome to take a look around." She waved her hand, gesturing vaguely to the shelving that lined the side wall of the shop.

"Great. Thanks." He moved to a display cabinet of ceramic bowls, picking up one in a deep sapphire blue and turning it in his hands. He studied it for what seemed to Juniper an unnecessarily long time. "You're very good at this."

His comment took her by surprise. She was good at it, had worked very hard to become so, but she hadn't expected him to recognize that fact. "Yes."

He looked up at her, assessing her for a moment. "It's for her birthday."

"Sorry?"

"The gift. For my mother. It's for her birthday."

"Oh. Lovely. What does she like?"

"I think I'd like to get her a flowerpot. But maybe something funny. She's got a really good sense of humor. I like to get her jokey sorts of presents."

Juniper thought for a moment. "I might have just the thing. Hang on a sec."

She moved through the beaded curtain and walked over to a table that housed her completed items. She knew Mikayla was watching her, but she refused to make eye contact.

"Is that William?"

"Mm hmm."

"Is William here? I've gotta show him my turtle." Before she could even draw breath, Billy had slid off the stool, purple turtle in hand. He dashed across the work room, through the beaded curtain, into the shop.

"I saw you at the beach," he announced upon entering the shop.

"So you did. I saw you, too."

"Mummy says you're special."

"Does she?"

Sweet Jesus, Juniper thought to herself.

"Yeah. Coz you helped me get born."

"Well, your Mum did most of the work."

"I made a turtle."

"Wow, that's amazing."

"But I can't think of a name for him."

"Myrtle."

Silence for a moment then Billy's giggle floated on the air. "Myrtle the Turtle. That's funny." Another long, quiet moment. Juniper could just picture Billy standing in the middle of the shop, giving William the once over. "I like you."

"I like you, too."

"Will you go to the beach with me one day? I like to build forts."

A moment of hesitation had Juniper's heart tightening in her chest. Billy was very sensitive, highly attuned to people. He'd recognize rejection and feel it deeply. "Sure."

She let out a breath of relief, grabbing what she'd come in for, and rushing back through the archway. "Billy, Mikky's got some crackers for you."

"Bye, William."

"Bye, Billy."

She held the curtain aside for him to walk through, his turtle clutched tight to his chest.

"How about this?" She placed it on the counter. It was a bright blue flowerpot, with *Sometimes I Wet My Plants* written on the side.

William laughed. "It's perfect. She'll love it. I'll take it."

"Lovely. Can I gift wrap it for you?"

"Yes, please."

"When's her birthday?"

"May."

"May? You shop early."

"Sure."

She looked up, as something in the tone of his voice caught her. She knew what came next. He was about to ask her out. But hot flushes and stuttering hearts notwithstanding, she didn't want to go on a date with him. Well, that wasn't exactly true. She did want to go on a date with him, but that would be getting into dangerous territory. Territory that she didn't have the strength to navigate. He was just too...everything. "I won't be a minute." She dashed back through the curtain, feeling a little frantic.

Mikayla, seeing the expression on Juniper's face as she returned, was on her feet in an instant. "What's up?"

"What? Nothing. I just need some more wrapping paper."

Mikayla glanced at Leah, studiously painting flowers on her plate and moved to Juniper's side. "What's up?" She asked again, in a low voice.

"He's going to ask me out."

Excellent! Mikayla thought. Her gorgeous friend deserved a hot date.

"No, don't look like that. I don't want to go on a date with him."

"Bullshit."

"Mikayla, please." She was looking edgy, desperate.

"Okay, fine." Mikayla surveyed her for a moment. "You look like an anxious teenager. Pull yourself together and play it cool." She pushed through the beaded curtain. "William! Hi! How great to see you again."

"Hi. It's great to see you too."

Holy smokes, he was gorgeous.

Juniper moved to the counter, unfolding the tissue paper and placing the pot in the center. "Sorry about that. Just had to grab some more paper."

"No problem."

"Great weather we're having." Mikayla leaned her hip on the counter and folded her arms across her chest.

"Yeah, it's lovely."

"Getting lots of work done?"

"Sure."

A long silence dragged out. Umm, what else? "Do you surf?"

"Not really."

Awkward. He couldn't have made it plainer that he didn't want her there, but he was being super polite about it. He also couldn't take his eyes of Juniper as he took the gift from her and handed over the cash. With a spurt of pure mischief, Mikayla said "Hey, if you're around on the weekend, you should check out the music festival."

"Yeah?"

"Yeah, you don't wanna miss it. Lots of bands playing, obviously. But there'll be food trucks and some stalls and fireworks after the sun sets."

"Sounds great."

"So, we'll see you there?"

He shrugged non-committedly, looking from Mikayla to Juniper and back again. He was trying to play it cool and failing spectacularly. Mikayla loved that in a man. "Sure, if I'm around."

"Great!" Mikayla said brightly.

"Thanks, Juniper." He held up the bag. "Mum will love it."

"You're welcome."

"Bye, then."

"Bye."

"Bye! See you Saturday!"

"Mikayla!" Juniper hissed once William had left.

She widened her eyes, the picture of innocence. "What? It's not a date."

"Some help you are," she grumbled as they walked back into the workroom.

"Rafael McKenzie! Get your hands off my cheese!"

"I bet you say that to all the boys."

"Funny." Mikayla sat down next to him, taking the cheese and cracker he was about to eat and popping it in her mouth. "What're you doing here?"

He gestured towards the Tupperware container in the middle of the table. "I was just at your Mum's and she wanted me to give these to Billy."

"As if Billy needs any more cookies." She ruffled Billy's hair as he grinned at her around a mouthful of choc chip cookie.

"A boy can never have too many cookies," Rafe stated.

"What a stupid thing to say. Of course, they can."

"Nah —"

"Children, children. I'm trying to run a business here," Juniper intervened, amused.

"Gotcha." Rafe got to his feet, looking at Mikayla as he took a handful of cookies and put them in his pocket, his dark eyes daring her to protest.

She rolled her eyes, laughing. "Seeya tonight."

"Seeya."

Once he was gone, Mikayla picked up her paintbrush and idly dipped it in the red paint. She looked up at Juniper, considering her for a long moment. She knew Juniper was aware of her scrutiny and was avoiding eye contact. "I'm really looking forward to the music festival." She glanced at Leah, with her head bent shyly over her work. Oh now, there's a plan. "Leah, you should come with us."

Leah looked up, startled. "Me?"

Mikayla, in her typical fashion, had taken to Leah on sight and was determined to befriend her. She looked very much in need of a good friend. "Yes, you! Don't bother saying no. I know where you live."

Leah laughed. "Alright, it sounds lovely."

"Excellent. Well, Juniper might already have a date lined up, but maybe you and I can get lucky."

Leah frowned with confusion. "You?"

"Ah yes, why not me?"

"Oh, because I thought you already had someone."

It was Mikayla's turn to frown with confusion. "Huh?"

"That guy that was just here."

Mikayla blinked at her then burst out laughing. "Rafe? God, no. He's my best mate but boyfriend, hell no!"

"Oh, I'm so sorry," Leah said, a faint blush staining her cheeks. "It's just that you seemed so..." She trailed off as Mikayla snorted.

"I've known him since we were seven years old. I love him to pieces but he's like a brother to me." She bit into a carrot stick. "So, now that we've got that straightened out, it's you and me, girl, on the prowl."

Leah laughed. "I'm not really in the market but I'll lend you moral support."

Mikayla sighed, ready to push the point but there was something in Leah's eyes that gave her pause. There was a flash of pain that immediately piqued Mikayla's protective instinct. She looked from Juniper to Leah and back again. She sure had her work cut out for her between these two women.

CHAPTER 2

*W*illiam stood at the sliding door of the little cottage next to the lighthouse. The work was coming along nicely. The kitchenette had been installed, the plumbing in the bathroom was almost done, there was a bit of plastering left to do, then the floors could be sanded and polished. It wasn't that far off from being very comfortable and perfectly livable. His parents thought he was a bit mad, staying at the cottage while all the work was being done rather than a hotel in town. But he loved it up at the lighthouse. It had a feeling of serenity, unlike anything he'd ever experienced, even with all the construction work going on. At night, when all the tradespeople had finished up for the day, it was just him, the rolling ocean and the night sky.

But today he didn't feel very peaceful. He felt confused, which was a very unusual and uncomfortable feeling for him. He'd never met anyone quite like Juniper before. If he showed an interest in a particular woman, he was used to it being enthusiastically reciprocated. That wasn't to say he was a player, far from it, but he liked women, liked dating, liked sex. He was also pretty good at recognizing when someone was interested in him. He thought he'd seen that interest in Juniper until she'd scurried away when he'd been on the brink of asking her out. Her obvious gorgeousness aside, there was just something about her that pulled at him, got inside his head, under his skin. If it hadn't been for Mikayla's enthusiastic suggestion about the music festival, he would have done his best to push it aside. So here he was, a little bewildered, a little deflated, getting ready to wander around a festival with hundreds of people, hoping to bump into a woman, that as far as he could tell, didn't want a bar of him. But that wasn't entirely true, was it? There'd been some interest there, hadn't there? He heaved a sigh and pushed his fingers through his hair in frustration before grabbing his keys and heading out the door.

After driving around for ten minutes, he finally found a car park right at the top of Main Street and even then, that was only because someone walking down from their house had invited him to use their driveway. The sky was dotted with little puffs of white clouds, the temperature hovered around a comfortable eighty degrees and a light breeze wafted in off the sea.

He walked into town and saw straight away that the little town of Blessed Inlet sure knew how to throw a music festival. All the retail shops were closed, but the cafes and ice cream shops were doing a roaring trade. As the main road was closed to vehicle traffic, hundreds of people were milling about, chatting, laughing, eating. He walked past Juniper's shop, noting it was shut up tight. He stopped at a café and grabbed a takeaway coffee before continuing his stroll down the street. A string quartet set up in the middle of the road got his attention. He leaned against a light pole to listen, recognizing one of his father's favorites, Clair de Lune. When the tune had finished, he moved on to where a troupe of belly dancers was gyrating, hips swinging and brightly colored scarves flying. After that came a group of Irish dancers. All kids, by the looks, skipping and jumping as the violins played. It was a crazy combination, all the different types of music, all the dancers, but it somehow worked. He moved on to where Main Street ended at a t-intersection with Beach Road. This was also shut to vehicle traffic, except for the food trucks. They lined the length of the road and seemed to provide any variety of food that could be imagined – pizza, Lebanese kebabs, Thai noodles. The scents were as eclectic as the sounds coming from Main Street. At that moment, a sound caught his attention, and he turned his head. A singer was sitting on a hay bale, leaning against the brick wall of the last shop on the strip. She was dressed in a long, flowing dress, crimson and gold, with a matching scarf tied around her head. Standing next to her was a man in worn jeans and a dark yellow shirt, strumming softly on a guitar. The lady was singing Ave Maria, her eyes closed, her voice soaring above the commotion. He moved closer, joining the small crowd gathered around her. As he listened, he looked down at his coffee cup, swirling the contents around, when a little blonde mop caught his eye. It was Billy, standing directly in front of the singer, his hands in the pockets of his navy-blue shorts, staring at her intently. William glanced around, looking for Juniper, but she wasn't nearby. The next best bet would be Mikayla or Rafe but he couldn't see them either. He moved forward, crouching down to Billy's level.

"Billy, what are you doing? Where's your Mum?" He whispered, but Billy just kept staring, seemingly mesmerized by the singer. William touched his shoulder and said the boy's name again, this time trying to put a bit more authority into the whisper. It worked. The spell was broken as Billy turned to look at him. The glaze in his eyes cleared and he grinned at William.

"Hi!"

"Hi yourself." He took Billy's hand and led him away from the crowd. "Where's your Mum?"

"That lady's colors were so white!" He exclaimed loudly.

"Were they?" William asked, despite having no idea what he was talking about.

"Yeah, it was very pretty."

"Mate, where's your Mum?" William crouched down, turning the boy to look at him, as he kept straining to watch the singer. The urgency in William's voice must have finally grabbed at Billy's awareness as he looked around.

"Don't know." His little face crumpled as he realized he couldn't see his mother anywhere. "I want my Mummy." He was on the verge of tears.

"It's okay, we'll find her."

"I want my Mummy!" Billy's big blue eyes welled with tears, and he threw himself at William, wrapping his arms around his neck. William picked him up and looked up and down the street. There were just so many people, the road was crowded, all the food trucks had lines ten people deep. Then he saw her, well, just the top of her head, blonde curls bobbing madly as she looked from side to side, pushing through the crowd.

"There she is!" With too many people between them and Juniper, William threw Billy up on his shoulder and pointed in Juniper's general direction. "Call out to her."

"Mummy! Mummy, over here!"

William saw her pause, looking around. "Again, buddy."

"Mummy!" Billy's whole body shook as he waved frantically. It worked, Juniper finally turning in their direction. Pushing through the crowd, she was there in no time, her face flushed, her eyes panicked, her hands full of drink bottles and curly potato on a stick. She practically threw everything at William as she reached up to Billy, pulling him off his shoulder, into her arms. With her son's arms around her neck, she buried her face in his hair, squeezing tight.

"Billy, you scared the life out of me! I didn't know where you were!"

Billy pulled back and kissed her on the cheek. "I'm sorry, Mummy. I wanted to see the lady singing."

"Well, don't do that again!" She took a deep, calming breath and turned to William. A radiant smile lit up her face, kicking him full in the guts. "Don't you just have a habit of turning up exactly when I need you."

He laughed, ignoring his heart, thudding hard against his ribcage. "So it seems." Then they just stood there, for the longest moment, smiling at each other.

"Mummy, can I please have my curly potato now?"

Juniper, startled, looked at Billy, then back at William. "Oh, sorry!" Putting Billy down, she took the drinks and the stick of curly potato from him. "I didn't mean to dump all that on you."

"No worries."

She put the drinks in her bag and handed the potato stick to Billy. "Let me just call the others and find out where they are." She kept the call brief and her grip tight on Billy's hand. "They've found a spot under a tree, on the grass behind the pizza truck." She started walking, pushing through the crowd again, clearly expecting him to follow her. As it was exactly what he wanted to do, and he happily complied.

They'd taken about four steps when Billy piped up. "Mummy, I can't see. Can William carry me?"

Before Juniper could reply, William said, "Sure. Just don't stab me with that stick." He lifted the little boy in his arms, feeling a spurt of surprise when Juniper took his hand in hers, pulling him through the crowd. It was slightly ridiculous, how good it felt to be walking along with her, holding hands. But it was short-lived, with Billy squirming to get down as soon as they made it to the grass and Juniper dropping William's hand, leaving him with a pang of regret.

"I got a curly potato!"

William was really starting to enjoy Billy's habit of announcing everything that happened to him.

"Wow, good one!" Mikayla grinned at him before transferring her smile to William. "William! You made it! Pull up some grass. This is Leah." She gestured to a petite brunette sitting next to her, who stood up to shake his hand, keeping her eyes downcast. "She's new in town, so we've gotta look after her. Here, try these." He'd barely sat down when Mikayla was shoving a full plate of food in his hands.

"Ah, thanks. What is it?"

"A bit of Polish, a bit of Lebanese, a bit of Thai. Rafe, the man needs a beer."

"Gotcha." Rafe reached behind him and grabbed a bottle from the icebox.

"Thanks."

William enjoyed lunch; the food was amazing and the company was better. Billy sat next to him, regaling him with all sorts of stories about his friends at playgroup, his favorite books, and his toys. Although he'd never had much experience with kids, he quite liked the idea of them and planned to have a few himself, one day. He had the strangest feeling, though, as he sat there listening to Billy's chatter. He, William, had helped him into the world. He'd cut the cord minutes after he'd been born. He felt a little overwhelmed, all of a sudden, a rush of something unfamiliar flooding him; A sense of connection so completely unexpected that it left him speechless. He gave himself a shake, forcing his mind to concentrate on what Billy was saying.

Then he was distracted by Juniper. "Honestly, you two, you're like an old married couple."

Mikayla snorted derisively.

"Well, you are!" Juniper insisted.

"I thought you were a couple," William admitted, immensely amused at Mikayla's exaggerated eye roll.

"People really have to stop saying that." Mikayla pushed at Rafe's shoulder, grinning at him as he shoved back.

They had a very comfortable, familiar dynamic, probably more affectionate than romantic, William thought. "How do you know each other?" He asked curiously.

"Ah, now there's a story. You tell him. You always tell it better." Mikayla lay back on the grass, hands behind her head.

With a smile, Rafe began, "I was seven years old and new in town. As scrawny as a rake and short, can you believe it?" It was hard to believe, since he was a towering figure now at over six foot three.

⁓

"*I*t's true. I was taller." Mikayla interjected. "But that didn't last long."

Rafe poked her in the ribs, grinning at her as she squirmed. "Anyway, I'd just started at Blessed Inlet Primary School and was having a rough time of it. I lived with my Abuela, my grandmother, and she didn't speak much English, so neither did I, at home. My skills were a bit rusty and there were some kids who didn't like it. Towards the end of my first week, I was miserable and angry and seriously ready to fight. I picked a fight with Andy Jenkins, the biggest and meanest of all the kids in the second grade. He knocked me down, I got up and swung a punch, missed, he knocked me down again. All the kids gathered around to watch me get beaten to a pulp, but Anne of Green Gables over here was having none of it." He looked at Mikayla, his eyes dancing. "I'll never forget it. I was on the ground, but I could see her storming across the playground. She yells, hey, *gilipollas*. Right pronunciation and everything."

"I'd been practicing," Mikayla interpolated with a grin.

"Andy turns around, confused and she just gut punches him. He falls like a ton of bricks, and she steps over him, leans down and grabs my shirt, pulling me to my feet." He fisted his hand in his shirt front to demonstrate. "Then she says, 'any of you arseholes touch my friend, you answer to me. Got it?' They all nod and she pulls me away, off to the nurse."

Juniper sighed. "I never get sick of hearing that story. You were a tough cookie back in the day, Sinclair."

"She sure was," Rafe said affectionately.

"And don't you forget it, *gilipollas*." They all laughed as Mikayla got to her feet, bending to pick up their rubbish. "Let's go, hey. The band will be starting soon."

They made quick work of the cleanup and were just about to move off when Mikayla said, "Shut the f—"

"Mikky!" Rafe interjected hastily.

"—ridge. The bastard!" She was off, bright red ponytail bouncing with each stride. They all watched as she headed down the footpath, then she called out, "Hey!" A man, who was leaning against the rock wall separating the path from the sand, looked up, straightening hastily as she approached. From where William stood, it looked like Mikayla was about to hit him, but then she ran the last few steps and threw her arms around his neck. The man, for his part, caught her adroitly and spun her around twice before setting her on her feet. When she found her feet, she placed both hands on the man's chest and shoved, hard.

"Who's that?" William asked. Mikayla now had the man by the hand and was dragging him up the path.

"Her brother," Juniper answered, in some amusement. As they approached, William was surprised to feel a small hand pulling on his. He looked down to see Billy looking at him anxiously. Going on instinct, he put his hands out, offering to pick him up.

Juniper watched as Billy raised his arms and William scooped him up. She knew he could be anxious when meeting new people, but she was fascinated that he would turn to William for reassurance. She didn't have time to follow that line of thought, however, because Mikayla had arrived, with her brother firmly in tow.

"William, Leah, this is my bastard of a brother, Callum, who has been away for two years and has returned today without so much as a text message to let me know."

"It was meant to be a surprise," he replied, shaking first William's hand, then Leah's. He gave Juniper a kiss on the cheek and hugged Rafe, affectionately slapping him on the back.

"Well, it was! Do Mum and Dad even know you're here?"

"Not yet. I parked at their place and walked down. I literally got in about ten minutes ago."

"They're probably at the pavilion. We were just heading there now, so let's go."

In her usual whirlwind fashion, Mikayla was off, pulling them all with her, except Leah. "You okay, honey?" Juniper asked. She looked like she'd seen a ghost. "Do you know Callum?"

"Ah, no, not really. I mean, um...no. No, I don't know him." She seemed to give herself a shake before mustering an uncertain smile. "We'd better catch up."

Juniper followed her with a perplexed frown. Although she didn't know Leah that well, from what she could tell, she was quite shy and maybe lacking in confidence. Callum was a famous musician so meeting him could certainly intimidate her, but it seemed more than that. There wasn't much she could do to help, though, so she just followed behind Leah as they caught up with the group.

The local sports oval had been repurposed into an outdoor music hall. A large marquee was at one end with a raised stage for the musicians and a dance floor laid out in front of it. Plastic tables and chairs were then scattered around at random, with tablecloths and flowers in glass jars on top.

"There they are!" Mikayla pointed to her parents, pushing Callum in their direction. Juniper couldn't help but smile at their reaction to seeing their prodigal son. She absolutely adored Mikayla's parents and almost thought of them like her own Mum and Dad. They had looked after her so much after Billy had been born and acted like surrogate grandparents to him. God knows, her own parents weren't at all interested, so to Juniper, Nora and John were an absolute blessing.

"William, hi."

"Hi, John."

"You two know each other?" Mikayla asked, the surprise in her tone obvious.

"We sure do. William's got my crew working like drovers up at the lighthouse," John replied with a wink.

William laughed. "They're a great crew, I certainly don't need to push them."

"Dad, do you know who William is?"

"Sure, poppet, he's the man who owns the lighthouse," John replied, with some confusion.

"He's also the man that stopped to help Juniper deliver Billy."

"Is he now?" Nora exclaimed. "Well, that deserves a hug." She stepped forward and pulled William into a tight embrace.

"Well, if I'd known that, I would've given you a discount on the job." John put his arm around Juniper's shoulders, pulling her against his side as he shook William's hand enthusiastically. "Words can't describe what you did for our girl."

Juniper smiled at the simple truth of the words, then she was intrigued to see that William looked a little uncomfortable.

"It was nothing, really."

"Not to me it wasn't," she said softly. He might be standing in front of her now in his fancy shoes and expensive sunglasses, all slick and smooth, but she knew who he really was. She almost laughed at herself for questioning it. The man that had held her that night, cradled in his arms, whispering soft words of encouragement, was the real William Locke. With a flash of insight, she knew that this William was a façade. She tilted her head to one side, a smile curving her lips. There was some digging to do here and looking at him, standing there with a soft ocean breeze playing with his hair, eyes clouded with confusion while he watched her watching him, she felt more than happy to pick up a spade and get digging.

"I think we need some more tables." John and Callum grabbed more tables and chairs, and everyone sat down to listen to the band. It was a Beatles cover band, belting out a great rendition of Twist and Shout. Juniper tapped her foot to the beat of the music as she watched people on the dance floor.

"You want to dance?"

She turned to William with a smile. "Sure." Rising to her feet, she checked with Nora. "You right with Billy?" He was sitting on her lap, wriggling his hips and clapping in time to the music.

"Of course. Off you go."

William took her hand, and they wended their way through the tables to the dance floor. They moved onto the floor just as the song finished and William turned her into him. She placed one hand on his shoulder, allowing him to take her other hand in his as he wrapped his arm around her waist. When the drumbeat dropped, the singer yelled the first line of "Can't Buy Me Love" into the microphone. Juniper felt William's grip tighten around her fingers, the slight pressure from his hand in the small of her back, she let her let instinct take over, shifting her weight to her right foot, then back to her left, dropping her right foot back as he stepped forward. She felt the flow immediately, the smooth way his hand pressed into her back, turning her where he wanted her to go.

"You can dance!"

He laughed. "So can you."

She surrendered to the beat and his hands, turning exactly as he wanted her to, spinning out and back in, then behind him, back around the front, back out again. He held her hand high above her head and she spun around twice before being pulled tight against him. She grinned up at him, recognizing the enjoyment in his eyes before he whirled her away again. Here was pure joy and she reveled in it. The song wound down, the singer crooning the last line of the song and on the final drumbeat, she wrapped her arm around William's neck as he dipped her. She laughed as he pulled her upright, hearing the crowd applauding.

"Give it up for Fred and Ginger, everyone."

She looked around, realizing the other dancers had formed a circle around them as they danced, and that the applause was for them. Laughing and breathless, she dropped a little curtsy as William bowed and grinned before taking her hand, and pulling her off the dance floor, through the crowd, back to their table.

"Wow, that was amazing!" Nora said enthusiastically, handing over a glass of chilled wine.

"Thank you." Juniper was still trying to catch her breath. It had been a very long time since she had danced like that, but God, she'd loved every second of it. She sat down, putting one arm around Billy as he climbed into her lap, holding her wine glass high so he didn't knock it.

Mikayla leaned over and whispered in her ear, "You know what they say about guys who can dance?"

She was almost too afraid to ask. "No, what?"

"They're amazing in bed."

She glanced at William, leaning back casually in his chair talking to Rafe and looking outrageously handsome.

"Hmm," was all she said.

Mikayla grinned, giving her arm a poke. "That's the way."

She watched him a moment longer, his long fingers wrapped around the neck of the beer bottle, laughing at something Rafe was saying. He glanced her way, their eyes met, she felt a little thrill, warm and enticing. Yes, there was definitely something worth exploring there, but she needed to dig under the slick first, just to be sure, before she dived in.

They spent the next few hours listening to the music, dancing every now and then, snacking and drinking from Nora and John's picnic basket.

As the sun faded from the day, pulling out all the warmth with it, Juniper reached into her backpack for a jumper for Billy and a cardigan for herself.

At that moment, Mikayla reached over and slapping Callum on the shoulder, gestured to the stage, saying, "You gonna get up there and give it a go?"

Juniper turned to him with a smile. She loved hearing him sing. She always turned the radio up when one of his songs came on, but there was no mistaking the shadow that passed over his face as he said, "Nah."

"What? Why not? It's free mic night after this next set. I haven't heard you play live in ages."

He shifted in his chair uncomfortably and shrugged his shoulders. "I'm not in the mood."

"Since when?" Mikayla snorted.

"Since now."

Mikayla stared at him for a long moment before shrugging and turning away, saying in a loud aside to Rafe, "No idea what's crawled up his ass."

"Mikky, leave it," John intoned, leaving Mikayla to slump grumpily in her chair.

Juniper watched Callum, staring down at his beer bottle, peeling at the label with frustration. The exchange left an awkward vibe in the air, broken by Nora's suggestion that they head to the beach for the fireworks. Billy's excited response had everyone laughing and went some way to relieving the tension.

As they walked across the road on the way to the beach, Juniper saw Mikayla sidle up to Callum and bump him with her hip, saying something to him earnestly. He shook his head and she bumped him again. As he turned his head to look at her, Juniper could see a smile pull at the corner of his mouth. He put his arm around her and pulled her close against his side, saying something in her ear that made her laugh out loud. Then he pulled away, shoving at her shoulder so that she stumbled into Rafe. She turned and threw a punch, her eyes alight with laughter.

Then they both cracked up when Nora stepped in, reaching up to slap Callum on the back of the head and telling him not to pick on his sister.

"They're a great family," William observed.

"They sure are." She glanced behind her to where Billy was walking along with Leah, holding her hand and telling her all about his friends at playgroup. "I couldn't have got on without them when Billy was born. They're the best."

"What about your own family?" He asked quietly.

She shrugged dismissively. "That's a story for another day." They reached the beach, forestalling any more conversation for the moment. They settled on picnic blankets under the glow of the faint crescent moon, which provided minimal light once the last of the sun's rays faded away.

Billy unceremoniously plopped himself down in William's lap, making himself right at home. "Okay?"

"Of course," William responded. That sort of ready acceptance of her child went an awful long way to answering any lingering questions Juniper may have had about William.

The first set of fireworks shot into the sky and the loud pop caused Billy to slap his hands over his ears. The colors burst across the sky, reflected in the rolling waves of the sea. She turned her head to look at Billy as he stared at the sky in wonder. William turned to look at her, the colors dancing across his face as more fireworks blasted into the air. His smile had her insides turning to mush.

"I'm glad you came."

"Me too," he said softly. He turned away, shifting Billy's weight in his lap before returning his attention to the light show.

Once the show was over, William offered to walk her home. It wasn't that far, but Billy was starting to lag, all the excitement of the day was finally catching up with him.

They said goodbye to the rest of the group, Juniper studiously ignoring Mikayla's exaggerated facial expressions as she hugged her. They walked up Main Street in companionable silence, Billy's head dropping onto William's shoulder more with each step they took. He was asleep before they turned into the gate that led around the back of the ceramics shop.

"Just through here," Juniper whispered as she walked across the yard. She pulled her phone out and turned on the torch app. "Watch your step. Billy has toys spread from one end of the yard to the other." She nudged a toy tractor aside with her toe before mounting the steps to her front door, pushing it open.

"You don't lock the door?" William whispered.

"No. Anyone that might break in was down at the beach watching the fireworks," she replied, barely disguising the faint chuckle in her voice.

"You realize that makes no sense, right? Tonight would be a perfect time to get into someone's house and take all their stuff."

"Not in Blessed Inlet," she replied confidently, leading him across her small lounge room, down the short hallway, into Billy's room. Switching on the night light, she pushed the duvet away and stepped back to allow William to lay Billy down. He did it so carefully and gently that she just had to smile again. "Wait for me." She kept her voice low as he stepped out, turning her head to catch his nod before he stepped out. She quickly settled Billy, taking his shoes and shorts off, slipping a night diaper on, pulling the duvet over him and searching around the bed for his soft toy lamb, placing that next to him on the pillow.

She folded her arms across her chest as she stepped out of Billy's room. The warm day had finished with a slight chill in the air. She saw through the lounge room window that William was out on the little deck near her front door. He turned as she came outside.

"This is a pretty good set up you've got here."

"I know. It's perfect for us." She looked around. The enclosed yard was reasonably large and well kept, disregarding the mess Billy left behind him wherever he went. A large oak provided enough shade for comfort in the height of summer. There was a breezeway that connected her little cottage to the backdoor of the shop, which led directly into her workroom. She was no more than a five-minute walk to the supermarket, post office, beach, and Nora and John's place. She turned back to William to find him looking at her.

"I have to go back to Sydney for a few days. When I get back, I'd really like to see you again."

"Like a date?"

"Yes, like a date."

She gave him a small smile, stepping forward so she was directly in front of him. His eyes never left her face. "There's something I want to check first." She placed one hand on his chest and stepping up on tiptoe, brushed her lips ever so lightly across his. She felt the tingle, the twinge of heat. Mmm, lovely.

"I have one condition."

He tilted his head, looking at her enquiringly.

"You can't spend more than fifty dollars."

He frowned, perplexed. "I can't spend more than fifty dollars?"

"That's right. You can't buy my love." She said, referencing the song they'd danced to at the festival.

His frown deepened. "I don't want to *buy* your love."

She touched his cheek, smiling her reassurance. He was clearly confused. "William, I've seen the men in your circle a million times. I'm not impressed by money. I don't want to be whisked off in a helicopter or private jet to some exotic location like they do in the movies. I just want to spend some time with you, getting to know you. The real you. If you're interested in that too, let me know when you get back and we'll have a date." She stepped back.

"I will." He was gone on the words, stepping carefully across the yard and through the gate.

Juniper touched her fingertips to her lips, smiling to herself as she went back inside.

CHAPTER 3

"*M*ummy, you look so pretty!"

Juniper turned her back to the mirror, looking over her shoulder, trying to get a good look at the back view. She was wearing a knee-length cream lace dress, that cinched in at the waist with a tan colored belt.

"Billy's on to it, girl. You look smokin'." Mikayla pulled a corn chip from the bag and bit into it with a loud crunch before holding the bag out to Leah.

Juniper looked at Leah uncertainly. She was the one with the most fashion skills. Leah dusted corn chip crumbs from her fingers and rose from her seat next to Mikayla at the foot of Juniper's bed. She moved to the wardrobe, the doors already hanging open and its contents trawled through. "Yes, that's the right dress, but you need..." she hunted around on the floor of the wardrobe "these!" She held a pair of tan colored sandals. "And I think you should wear your hair down."

"Really? I think it's a bit more formal if I pull it up like this?"

"Exactly."

She surveyed herself in the mirror again and sighed. "I hate not knowing where he's taking me. I don't know how to dress for it."

"He said casual and it's a day date, so hair out, that dress, these shoes." Leah moved to the jewelry box on the dressing table and riffled through. "And these earrings. Perfect."

She'd just tied the strap on her sandal when she heard the knock at the front door. Her heart thudded uncomfortably, and she felt strangely nervous. "Oh God, he's here." She hastily pulled the pins out of her hair and fluffed at it, trying to get it to sit right.

"Relax, you look great." Mikayla crunched on another corn chip as she got to her feet. "Super hot guy who's seriously got the hots for you is taking you someplace unknown to do God-knows-what with you. What's to stress about?"

Juniper laughed, which eased her nerves a little. Taking a deep breath, she said, "You're right. Of course, you're right." She smoothed her hands down the front of the dress, grabbed her handbag from the dressing table, and went to answer the door. She'd just pulled it open when Billy snuck out from behind her.

"William! I'm eating corn chips!"

"Are you buddy? That's great."

"You want some?"

"Ah, no thanks." He was dressed in beige cargo shorts, a light blue linen button down shirt and loafers. Phew, she was dressed appropriately. "I've got something for you though, if your Mum says you can have it." He was holding one hand behind his back, so with the other, he reached into his pocket and took out a chuppa chup. He looked at Juniper with a brow raised in inquiry. She gave the go ahead and he handed it over to Billy.

"What do you say?" She said warningly when Billy moved to run away.

"Thanks!" And he was off. "Mikky! William gave me a lollypop!"

"I've got something for you too." Pulling his arm from behind his back, he presented her with a bunch of sunflowers.

"Oh, my favorite! How did you know?"

"I didn't. I just picked them from the patch at your front fence. Didn't want to blow any of my budget on flowers."

She laughed. "Thank you, they're lovely."

"I'll take those, so you guys can get going." Mikayla appeared next to her, grabbing the flowers from her hands and heading to the kitchen for a vase.

"Oh, okay. Thanks. Bye, Leah, thanks for your help!"

"No worries!" Leah called from the bedroom, where she was studiously reorganizing the wardrobe.

"You kids have fun now," Mikayla said from the kitchen.

"Thanks. Bye, Billy!"

"Bye, Mum!"

"Good to know he's devastated about me leaving him," she joked as they stepped off the porch and across the lawn. "So, where are we off to?"

"It's a surprise." He opened the passenger door of the Porsche, stepping aside so she could get in. "You look lovely, by the way."

"Thank you." She slid into the seat, smiling up at him as he closed the door.

"So far, I'm down fifty cents out of the allocated budget," he said as he got in beside her. "The lollypop," he answered with a smile when he saw her inquiring look.

"How're you doing for the rest of it?"

"Pretty good." He backed the car out of the driveway, swinging out onto Main Street and heading out of town.

"Hmm, not somewhere in town then."

He just smiled in response.

William drove for a little while, following the road that met up with the highway. "Do you think I'm money hungry?"

He felt her looking at him with surprise. "No, not really."

He pondered for a moment. "Then why the budget?"

She was silent for so long he thought she wasn't going to answer. "Because I think you have a way of relating to your money that's covering up part of you that I want to know more about."

He frowned in confusion. *What the hell did she mean by that?*

"I'm sorry if I've offended you."

He drew a deep breath. "I'm not offended. I'm just not sure I understand you."

"I don't know how to say it without sounding rude."

"Just say it then."

Another long pause followed. "Everyone's got issues, right?"

He nodded. "I guess."

"Well, my issue is that my family is quite wealthy and quite flashy with it. Money and image are very important to them. I've never really fit that image. I've always been too much of something or not enough of something else. Having Billy on my own was the last straw for them. I haven't spoken to my parents or my sister at all since I left Melbourne." She stopped talking for a moment, staring through the windscreen. He could see her throat working as she tried to hold back tears. "It hurt me a lot. I spent many years trying to fit in, but I can't change who I am. You remind me a lot of the people in that circle. To be perfectly honest with you, if that day on the beach was the first time I'd met you, I wouldn't have looked twice at you. But it wasn't the first time, so I see you differently. I remember what you were like the night I had Billy and I want to know more about that person. Because I like that person. A lot."

He had absolutely no idea how to respond to any of that, so he didn't say anything. He'd just stick with the last bit. She liked him.

They were both quiet as he continued up the road, neither speaking as he turned the car into a gravel side road and eased carefully down it until they reached a long, low mud brick building with the words *Maison des Papillons* inscribed in big, swirling letters on a sign above the door. He just smiled at Juniper as she looked at him inquiringly and got out of the car.

"Oooh!" She exclaimed when he opened the door for her to pass through, into the ticket office. "Butterflies!" She looked around, wide eyed, then she turned to him with a huge smile on her face and he knew he'd nailed it.

"Bonjour!" A woman came in from an office out the back, short and round with wild curly brown hair pulled back with a multicolored scarf. "You want to see the butterflies, yes?"

"We sure do."

"Ten dollars each, please." He handed over the cash and received a brochure in return, with tickets and instructions on where to go.

"Twenty dollars and fifty cents down," William said as they walked through an archway, then out a double-glazed glass door into an enormous butterfly enclosure.

"Tell me, what would you have organized if I hadn't put a budget on our first date?"

He thought for a moment and had to admit, he would have gone overboard. "A helicopter ride somewhere, a swanky restaurant on a rooftop terrace with crap music and expensive wine."

She laughed. "See, this is better, isn't it?"

He watched her for a long moment as she looked around, her curls going wild in the humid air. "Yeah, this is better."

She brought her gaze back to his, with a small smile curving her lips. "Just to let you know, I'm going to be very disappointed if you haven't kissed me by the time we get to the end of this walk." She turned and strolled off on the words, down the wooden ramp, into the lush foliage. He followed, and a little thrill of anticipation made his heart tighten in his chest.

Juniper heard his footsteps behind her and waited for him to catch up, slipping her hand in his as they walked on. They paused here and there to watch the butterflies as they danced about above their heads. She hoped she hadn't upset him in the car. He didn't seem upset, but he didn't seem exactly happy, either. He was just so...quiet. She felt a little sad about it, but also felt it was better to be honest and upfront with him. She paused by a wooden railing to watch a particularly stunning butterfly fluttering about, the blue of its wings so vivid and beautiful it almost brought tears to her eyes. It fluttered closer, hovering just near her face. She turned her head very slowly, wanting to make sure William was watching it too. Then it landed ever so lightly in her hair and she went utterly still, barely restraining a gasp of delight. She let the moment spin out, not sure how long butterflies liked to lie around in people's hair. "What is it doing?" She whispered.

"I don't know. Laying eggs?" He whispered back, his eyes dancing mischievously.

"Butterflies don't lay eggs."

"I know, which is lucky for you, because she looks like she's settled in for the long haul. Do you want me to get her out?"

"Yes."

He reached up and very gently slid his finger into her hair, pushing at the butterfly. It rested on the tip of his finger for a moment, wings flapping gently, before lifting off and fluttering back into the foliage. Juniper linked her fingers with his and walked on. As they rounded the final corner, she felt him tug at her hand and she turned back, looking at him inquiringly. He tugged again and she took two steps forward, until they were almost touching. She raised her gaze to his face, feeling a little shiver at the heat she saw swirling in the brandy-colored depths of his eyes. He lowered his head, ever so slowly, watching her.

She leaned into him, letting her eyes drift closed as his lips found hers, brushing softly, gently. Then he increased the pressure, and she opened her lips, sighing as she felt his tongue tangled with hers. She wound her arms around his neck, felt his arms come around her and she was pulled tight against him as he deepened the kiss with long, languorous strokes of his tongue. The heat pooled in her belly, and she sighed again, luxuriating in the pure pleasure of it. Then he slowly lifted his head and she let her eyes drift open, gazing up at him for a long moment before saying, "Hmm, lovely."

He chuckled. "Thanks." He reached up and pushed a golden curl back from her face. "You ready for what comes next?"

"That depends on what it is."

He grinned. "You'll see." He took her hand again and led her out to the car, then they were cruising back down the road, towards Blessed Inlet. He bypassed the town, taking the steep, curving track up to the lighthouse, driving around a triangular patch of stubby grass to park in front of one of the smaller buildings, closest to the towering lighthouse. She got out of the car and had a good look around. The sandstone buildings squatted in the high summer sun, their red, iron roofs shimmering in the heat. There were a few buildings of varying sizes dotted around and she wondered what they were all for.

"Would you like to have a look around?"

"Yes, definitely."

She followed him down the gravel drive and across more brittle grass towards a tall building. She stepped inside the open cavity onto flagstones and into the cool shadow. She looked up at the soaring ceilings and the sectioned space. "Stables?"

"Yes. It had become a bit of a dumping ground, so it was a bit of a job to clean it out, but it's got great bones."

"What will you use it for?"

"Evening functions."

She could see that quite easily, the space filled with people in fancy suits and dresses, milling about, snacking on delicate canapes while they schmoozed. It was a bit depressing, so she wandered out into the hot sunshine, heading towards the long, low building at the bottom edge of the compound. William opened the thick wooden door but stopped her from stepping inside. "The floor's not safe."

She peered into the dusty gloom, looking at the wide-open space. "This'll be the conference and team building area."

"Correct."

The next building had been the lighthouse keeper's cottage and was in similar condition to the conference center. Evidence of John's work was everywhere, from the sawhorses with long planks of flooring resting on them to the window frames neatly stacked against the wall.

William led the way to a small cottage closest to the cliff, nestled in the shadow of the lighthouse. Curious, she followed him inside. A lot of work had been done here.

"They've been hard at work here."

"Yeah, they concentrated on this first so I could stay here. It's fully functional now and will be the manager's residence. It's good to try it out and the view's amazing."

The front door opened into a little entrance foyer, which in turn opened onto a comfortable seating area, with two large, comfortable sofas that offered sweeping views of the rolling sea. To her right was a little kitchenette that overlooked a compact dining area, beyond that was a short hallway with a bedroom or two. The whole wall in front of the seating area had been given over to glass sliding doors that led out onto a sandstone patio. The whole place screamed elegance and comfort. She was impressed. William had moved into the kitchen, retrieving a picnic basket and a bottle of wine in a champagne bucket.

"This way."

She followed him out through the sliding doors, over the grass to the old, wooden door of the lighthouse. He placed the basket and bucket down between his feet and heaved the door open, gesturing her to go ahead of him up the narrow, spiral staircase. The stairs opened out to a narrow, beamed platform, where, to Juniper's utter delight, a table and chairs were tucked under the wide window. It was set for two with a white plastic tablecloth, plates, cutlery, wine glasses and a bunch of yellow daisies in a vase. She looked at William and saw him watching her with uncertainty. "I love it. It's perfect." She looked out across the ocean, the white caps of the waves, the gulls circling, the little town nestled in the curve of the beach. "Wow."

"It's something, isn't it?"

"It's amazing."

"Hungry?"

"A little."

She sat down, more than intrigued when he sat opposite her and placed the bucket and basket on the ground next to him.

"Right, so confession time. I love wine and I can't cook for peanuts, so this part was extra challenging." He opened the wine and poured for her first. She took a sip and nodded her approval. "Great, that's the best seven dollars I've ever spent."

She laughed. Next, he took out two containers and put them in the middle of the table. "Salmon frittata and a green salad." He removed the lids and served her a generous portion. She waited until he had served himself before she lifted her fork and took a bite.

"Mm, delicious."

"It's from Coco's."

"They do great food. You chose well. A toast." She lifted her wine glass and held it out, waiting for him to do the same, then clinked her glass gently against his. "To cheap dates."

He laughed. "To cheap dates."

They ate in companionable silence for a while. "Tell me about your family," Juniper said, after taking a sip of wine.

"There's not much to tell. It's just my Mum and Dad, me and my sister."

"What are their names?"

"Dad's Robert, Mum's Gwen and my sister is Cassandra, but we call her Cassie."

"You're close?"

He gave it some thought, then nodded. "We are close, but to be honest, I don't think about it that much. I guess I just take it for granted. I shouldn't. It scared the shit out of all of us when Dad had the stroke."

"I can imagine."

"Yeah, but he pulled through and he's doing okay, so I forget sometimes how terrifying it was."

"What about your Mum?"

"She's a rock. She runs the whole show and always has been, even before Dad got sick."

"And Cassie?"

"Hmm, Cassie." He pondered for a moment, a faraway look in his eye. "She's got Dad's business acumen and Mum's take no prisoners attitude. Nothing gets by her. She's fiercely loyal and protective. You cross someone she loves and she'll squash you flat."

"She sounds amazing."

"Yeah, but she's my baby sister so she still gives me the shits every other day."

Juniper laughed. "Fair enough."

"What about you, Juniper? You've mentioned your family. What about Billy's Dad?"

"Well, that's a bit of a weird story." She leaned back in her chair, taking a sip of wine and holding onto the glass as she gazed out at the ocean for a long moment. It was a weird story, and he might not like it, might judge her. She weighed up the options. She decided that if he was going to judge her, she'd rather know now than later. "My late twenties precipitated a bit of a crisis for me. A lot of things were coming to a head with my family, my work wasn't fulfilling me anymore and I just had a feeling that something was missing, that there had to be something more to life than this." She paused, considering how best to explain it.

"I know the feeling," he said softly, surprising her.

"Really?"

"Yes, but back to you."

"Right. Well, I started feeling like the *something more* might be a baby. Once I got the idea in my head, I couldn't let it go. It just grew and grew. So, I started seriously looking around for someone I could marry that would give me a baby. That seems so ridiculous now that I'm doing it on my own, but I was still tied to my family's expectations so at first that seemed the obvious solution."

"That makes sense."

"But there was just no one I could imagine being with in that way. Then one day I went to a Celtic festival, and I saw this man, and I just got this feeling. This flash of rock-hard certainty. This was it. This was exactly how I should do it. So, I approached him." She paused, searching his face, but it was shuttered, impassive. She took another sip of wine, feeling a little niggle of nervousness. "We talked for a little while, then I just came out with it. I just told him what I wanted. And he agreed."

"Just like that?"

"Just like that. I said I had no interest in a relationship, but he could be as involved as he liked. He said he wasn't ready to be a dad, his lifestyle didn't really allow it. But I've got his phone number, so if ever Billy wants to get in touch with him, he can."

"He doesn't ask?"

"Not yet. Maybe he's still too young. But he's got Mikayla and Rafe, and John and Nora. They're his family. Maybe he just doesn't want for more." She stopped then, looking at him, trying to gauge his reaction. Pure nervousness washed over her as she realized that her reasoning before, was based on false bravado. It mattered that he not judge her. So much more than she could have imagined even a few minutes earlier.

"I think you're amazing."

She let out an explosive breath. "Really?"

"God yes. What a thing to do, on your own. And Christ, you can hardly look at Billy and think he was a mistake."

She put a hand over her heart, where it was squeezing painfully. She couldn't control the tears that welled in her eyes and spilled down her cheeks.

"Hey," he said, softly. She rose hastily to her feet, rounding the table and before he had the chance to do the same, was in his lap, her arms around his neck, her face buried in his shoulder. His arms came around her, holding tight.

She stayed there for a little while, basking in the feel of his body against her, of the relief that had flooded her at his reaction. She pulled back to look at him, wiping at the tears on her face. "It matters to me that you think that." Then she pressed a soft kiss to his lips, but he pulled back before she could deepen it.

"Why would I not think that?"

She reached up and with the tip of her index finger, rubbed at the furrow between his brows. She'd hurt his feelings. "I can't explain to you how it was with my family when I told them. It was awful. They were awful. So, I'm a little sensitive about it. I'm sorry."

"Fair enough." He kissed her again before saying, "You know what you need?"

"What?"

"Dessert."

"Yes!" She moved to get off his lap, but he tightened his grip around her waist.

"You can have it where you are." He reached down into the picnic basket and pulled out two chuppa chups. "We've got strawberries and cream or coca cola. Lady's choice."

She laughed, delighted. "Budget didn't stretch to dessert?"

"You got it."

"Strawberries and cream, please." She worked the wrapper off then looked at him quizzically. "You're giving me a lollypop without making any rude jokes?"

"I'm a responsible, mature adult. I'm sure I can handle it."

He watched as she put the lollypop in her mouth and sucked. "Hmm, it's not very big."

"Jesus."

She was so gloriously unexpected, sitting in his lap, her eyes dancing with mischief. She gazed out at the ocean as she sucked on the lollypop and for the moment, he was content just to be with her, holding her. The moment spun out for an eternity. The cool breeze played with her hair. Her scent surrounded him, earthy and fresh. He just wanted to start kissing her and never stop. As if reading his mind, she dropped the half-eaten lollypop on his plate and wrapping both arms around his neck. She laid her lips over his. Her tongue was in his mouth, tasting of strawberries and cream chupa chup and pure heat. He ran his hands up and down her back, wanting more, needing more. She sighed, shifting a little, trying to get closer. He broke away, but only long enough to press hot, desperate kisses along her jawline. She tilted her head to give him better access as he found her earlobe, grazing it with his teeth and delighting in the shiver that went through her. He left a trail of kisses down her neck to her collarbone, but the dress was in the way, so he made his way back up to her lips, claiming them in a deep, drugging kiss. His fingers itched to touch flesh, so he slid his hand down over her hip, down to the hem of her lacey dress, and under. His fingers brushed against the soft, satiny skin of her thigh. She had one hand around his neck, the other roaming over his chest, then lower. If she went any further, he knew he was absolutely done for, so he hastily pulled his wandering hand out from under her dress and grabbed her wrist.

"We'd better stop."

"Yes." But she pulled away from his grip and buried her fingers in his hair, kissing him deeply, hungrily.

"Juniper," he said against her lips.

"I know."

"Not here. Not like this."

"No." She sighed and broke the kiss, resting her forehead against his, her breath shallow. "You'd better take me home."

"Okay." He smiled as she got to her feet with obvious reluctance, then blew out a sharp breath as he stood up. Christ, the woman could kiss.

*J*uniper brushed the hair back from her forehead with the back of her hand. She had wet clay all over her hands and an errant curl causing trouble. Seeing her, Mikayla came over and tucked it under the multi-colored scarf she had wrapped around her head. "Thanks."

"Then what did he say?"

Juniper's eyes got misty as she worked the clay around the wheel. "He said that you couldn't look at Billy and think he was a mistake."

"God, that is so hot," Leah said with a smile. "He's not wrong though," she quietly added from her seat at the wide workbench.

"Thank you," Juniper said, smiling at her. She took her foot off the pedal of the wheel to watch Leah for a moment, with a thoughtful frown on her face. Leah was intensely focused as she bent over a pale blue vase, tracing an outline of a poppy in delicate gold paint. She was extremely talented and watching her, Juniper's mind started to turn. She glanced at Mikayla who was looking from her to Leah and back again, her brow quirked in inquiry. Juniper sent her a small smile before pressing down on the pedal of the wheel again.

"When are you going to bang him?"

Juniper rolled her eyes. "Mikayla Sinclair, you have a one-track mind."

"I sure do and right now, that track is leading right to you having a night of unbridled passion." Her brown eyes glinting with mischief, Mikayla moved to the fridge and took out a can of coke, shooting a questioning look at Juniper, seeing her nod and grabbing one for her. "Coke, Leah?"

As she didn't answer, they both looked over. She was absolutely absorbed in her work now, oblivious to her surroundings. Mikayla grabbed a coke for her and took it over, sitting down to watch her as she worked. She glanced up at Juniper, who nodded in response. She had a plan brewing for Leah, she just needed the right moment to pull it together. Leah held the vase away from herself for a moment, studying it closely then nodding to herself. As she placed it gently on the table, she looked surprised when Mikayla pushed the coke towards her. She had been someplace else entirely. "Sorry, what was that?"

"Oh nothing, I was just wondering when our little Junebug was going to bang William."

Now it was Leah's turn to roll her eyes. "You have sex on the brain."

"Ha!" Juniper exclaimed. "See!"

"I'm not ashamed to admit it. You're the only one of us with a chance of getting any, so we gotta live vicariously through you."

Leah took a sip of coke. "I don't get what the fuss is about."

Mikayla stared at her wide eyed. "Get out of town."

Leah shrugged but a shadow passed over her face as she reached for the paintbrush and idly swirled it through the gold paint on her palette. Mikayla and Juniper exchanged glances before wordlessly agreeing to leave it.

"Mikky, can you check on Billy for me?"

"Sure." Mikayla walked to the back door. "He's in the sandpit."

"Great, thanks."

"Don't go thinking that gets you off the hook, though. I want a schedule."

Juniper looked at her with a puzzled expression.

"A banging schedule," Mikayla clarified.

Juniper laughed. "I don't know. I've got Billy to account for and William's back and forth to Sydney and wherever else he goes off to. I'll know when the time is right, and you'll be the first to know. Or maybe the second. I should probably let William know."

Obviously realizing that was all she was going to get out of Juniper, Mikayla, glancing at her watch, said, "I'd better get going. I gotta be at work in an hour."

"Okay."

Mikayla grabbed her bag and as she walked past Leah, stopped and wrapped her arms around her from behind. Juniper smiled. Leah seemed to need it and Mikayla, ever affectionate, was just the one to give it to her.

Juniper took the bowl she'd just thrown and placed it carefully on the shelf behind her. Then washing her hands in the basin, she grabbed her coke and moved to sit at the workbench with Leah.

"I want to talk to you."

Leah looked up nervously.

"I hope you'll like what I have to say," Juniper said reassuringly.

"Alright."

"I'm not quite sure how to say it so I'll just be blunt. I want you to work with me."

"Oh."

"I mean, what are you doing with all the pots, plates, vases and mugs you've painted?"

Leah smiled. "They're on the floor in my loungeroom because I have nowhere to keep them."

"Right, so at the moment you're paying me for the privilege of painting my stuff, plus, you're looking for work. It just doesn't make sense." Juniper paused, trying to get her thoughts in line. Suddenly, this felt very important, and she didn't want to mess it up. "I've been toying with the idea of developing my online shop for a while now, but I keep getting blocked by the idea that I can't produce the volume I'd want to for it to be worth it. I know it's a hobby for you and if you think doing it more professionally would spoil the pleasure of it, then don't do it. But honestly, Leah, I've never seen anyone who can paint pottery like you can." She tilted her head to one side as Leah's eyes welled with tears. "You don't like the idea?"

"I love it," Leah whispered around the lump in her throat.

"Oh, I'm so pleased!" Juniper threw her arms around her, giving her a tight hug. When she pulled back, they smiled at each other. "So, you're going to have to haul all those pots, plates, vases and mugs back here so we can sell them."

Leah laughed. "Alright!"

Juniper turned as she heard Billy reaching up to open the door. "Hey, what's up baby?" She went to him immediately.

"My head hurts," he said miserably.

She lifted him up, pressing her lips to his forehead. "Hmm, you've got a temperature." She looked over at Leah. "I need to take him inside and put him to bed."

"Of course. I can watch the shop if you like." She glanced at her watch. "It's only just over an hour til closing time anyway."

"Great, thank you so much." Juniper stroked Billy's head as he rested it on her shoulder. She had a feeling she was going to be in for a hard couple of days.

CHAPTER 4

 $\mathcal{W}$ illiam knocked on the door of Juniper's little cottage. They hadn't seen each other since their date to the butterfly enclosure, because he'd been caught up with work and Billy had been unwell. He felt a surge of anticipation at seeing her again, at maybe sneaking in an opportunity to kiss her. She hadn't answered the door, so he knocked again, then frowned as he heard shuffling around inside, a violent sneeze, then an irritable Juniper saying to Billy, "Baby, don't do that, please." She opened the door and he realized straight away that there would be no kissing today. She looked like death, warmed up, pale and bedraggled, still in her pajamas.

"William!" Her voice was husky and she coughed on the word. "I'm so sorry. I completely forgot we were catching up today."

"William! I'm playing with playdough!" Billy appeared at Juniper's side and grabbed William's hand, trying to pull him through the doorway.

"I'm not sure you want to come in here. It's a den of sickness."
As if to prove her words, Juniper turned away to sneeze into a
tissue.

"That's okay, I never get sick."

"Enter at your own risk then."

She stood back to allow him to enter before moving to the over-
stuffed armchair near the window and curling into it, leaning
her head back and closing her eyes. She looked absolutely miserable. "Why don't you go and have a lie down?"

"Can't. Billy."

"I can watch him for a bit."

It said something about how terrible she must be feeling that she
didn't protest, just got up and walked into the bedroom with a
mumbled, "thanks so much," and closed the door.

William turned to Billy, ensconced at the dining room table
with piles of playdough and cutouts spread across the top. "It's
just you and me then, buddy. What are we gonna do?" Billy
held up dinosaur shaped cookie cutters in response. "Okay then,
playdough it is."

They passed a good twenty minutes with William passing Billy
the tools he needed to make his playdough dinosaur park but
then the little boy started getting rowdy, making dinosaur noises
as he played and smashing the plastic molds around. No amount
of protest from William to keep the noise down made any difference. Billy would settle down for a little while, then the game
would get too much for him and he'd get louder and louder. As
if to prove William's point, Juniper came out of her room, shuffling slowly to the kitchen. William pushed to his feet, hurrying

to the sink to get her a drink. She smiled her thanks as she took it, sipping tentatively.

"God, my throat feels like it's on fire." She put the glass down and just stood there, swaying slightly. William took a half step forward and pulled her against him, gently rubbing her back. She let her head fall on his chest with a sigh.

"I thought I could get Billy out of the house for a few hours. Maybe take him to the beach so you can get a proper rest?" He asked softly so that Billy couldn't hear.

She pulled back, managing a small smile. "Sexier words have never been spoken."

"Hey, mate, you wanna go to the beach?" Billy indicated strongly in the affirmative by clapping his hands loudly and dashing off to his room to get his hat. Juniper moved to follow him, but William grabbed her arm and steered her towards her bedroom. "I can get everything he needs."

"Okay. His bag's in the wardrobe, sandals on his shoe shelf and the sunscreen is in the side pocket of his bag. He can get his drink bottle himself. Just make him go to the toilet before you head out."

They were out the door in under five minutes. William hustled to keep up with Billy as he raced across the lawn towards the gate.

"Take it easy, mate. You gotta hold my hand until we get to the beach." William only felt slightly ridiculous strolling down the street with a Bluey backpack slung over his shoulder. Honestly, the things a man was prepared to do for the woman he...liked. A lot.

The first hour of play went pretty well. The day was warm without being too hot, the sky clear and bright. Being a weekday, the beach wasn't too crowded, the seagulls being the main occupants. William was helping Billy pile damp sand as high as it could go when Billy suddenly pushed to his feet, with a mulish frown on his face, and kicked the top off the sandcastle.

"Hey!" William exclaimed, brushing sand off his shorts. Billy kicked again then jumped on the castle, flattening it. "What are you doing?"

"Sandcastles are stupid!"

"Well, you could have said that before we spent the better part of an hour building one!" William was confused. It seemed so out of character for Billy to throw a tantrum and as far as he could tell, it had come entirely out of the blue. "Stop doing that!"

"You can't tell me what to do!" Billy replied, giving the sand a hard kick in William's direction.

"Yes, I can!"

"Just coz you love Mummy, doesn't mean you're the boss of me!"

William was struck speechless. He sputtered; his mind was absolutely blank. All he could manage was, "What are you talking about?"

"I can see it in your colors." Billy plopped down on his bottom, crossed his arms and glared at William, his angelic face a picture of obstinacy.

William pushed his fingers through his hair, more than a little overwhelmed. "What would you know about it, you're not even three years old."

They had a stare off for a long moment, William totally clueless on what he should do next. Then to his relief, Billy's face crumpled, and he looked down at his feet. "I'm sorry," he whispered.

"Okay."

Billy looked up through his lashes, tears welling in his eyes. "Don't be cross."

"I'm not cross."

"Yes, you are."

"Maybe a little. Come here."

Billy scrambled to his feet and jumped forward, throwing himself into William's arms.

"You know what we need?"

"What?" The boy asked, his face pressed against William's neck.

"Ice cream."

"Oooh yeah!" Billy jumped to his feet, grabbed his sun hat and jammed it on his blonde curls. "Let's go."

"Hey, what are the rules?"

"I gotta hold your hand."

"That's right, so wait up."

Harmony restored, they walked across the footpath and over the road, but instead of heading up the Main Street, Billy pulled William's hand.

"Ice cream shop's up here, buddy."

"I don't feel like ice cream."

"Really? Because two minutes ago you couldn't get enough of the idea."

Billy shrugged and tugged on William's hand. Curious to see where they were headed and figuring the longer they spent out of the house, the more chance Juniper had to rest, William allowed Billy to lead the way. They turned left into the next street off Beach Road, then took the second street on the right. William looked around. He couldn't figure out where they were going, until Billy stopped in front of a two-story red brick home with a large front yard and a long driveway that led back to an enormous shed.

"Nora has cookies."

"You little brat! I'm not knocking on Nora's door demanding cookies. I barely know her."

"She'll make you tea and then you know her."

Well, that was a point that was hard to argue against. But still. "No, buddy. Let's go and have ice cream." Just as Billy's shoulders were slumping and his lip beginning to wobble, John came out to the door of the shed and called out.

"Hey, young fella. What're you doing here?"

"Nora has cookies," he stated, walking down the drive toward John.

"That she does. If you ask real nice, and use your manners, she might give you one."

Billy looked up at William triumphantly. "See!" he whispered in a loud aside.

"You're a scoundrel."

Billy grinned, delighted at the insult. Then he walked off, hands in his pockets, saying "scoundrel, scoooundrel, scoundrelll" to himself as he climbed the back steps and reached up on tiptoes to pull on the door handle. "Nora! I'm a scoundrel!" he shouted as he went inside.

"I've often said that," William heard Nora call back then both men smiled as Billy's giggle floated on the air.

William briefly explained how they'd ended up on John's doorstep demanding cookies, much to John's amusement. "He sure is a scallywag, but we wouldn't have him any other way."

"True." William followed John as he went back into the shed, dropping Billy's backpack onto the wide workbench. "This is a great setup you've got here."

"Yeah, it does the job. Cuppa?"

"Sure, thanks."

John moved to a bench against the back wall. Filling the kettle up at the sink, he said, "So, Juniper's not well?"

"No. She's caught what Billy had, apparently."

As the kettle boiled, John turned and leaned back against the counter, surveying William. There was an unmistakably parental glint in his eye that had William swallowing convulsively. "And you're just looking out for her, are you?"

"Something like that."

John watched him a moment longer then turned to get mugs from the cupboard. "Good," was all he said. The screen door into the house crashed open, and the sound of Billy's sandals slapping on the pavement could be heard. Then Billy appeared, hugging a Tupperware container to his chest.

"I got cookies, but Nora said you can only have two." He studiously handed the container to John, watching as he removed four cookies and put them on a plate, placing the lid back on the container. Satisfied that Nora's dictum was being adhered to, Billy moved to a low table that was covered in plastic tools. He plonked himself down in the chair and picked up a toy drill. "I've gotta finish making the house." It was abundantly clear that he spent a lot of time here and thoroughly enjoyed himself.

John made the tea, then took his, saying, "I just have to make a quick phone call. You're okay here?"

"Sure."

With Billy settled at his own little workbench, William was left to wander around at will. There was a large bin full of wooden offcuts from John's latest project. William picked up a small piece, weighed it in his hand, discarded it, reached for another. Once he found the right piece, he looked around and sure enough, on the shelf attached to the wall, there was a set of wood cutting knives. He picked up a whittling knife and, moving back to Billy's side of the shed, he leaned against the wall and, crossing one foot in front of the other, started working at the block of wood. He kept one ear cocked for Billy's chatter but as he sliced the knife into the wood, shaving away at it here and there, working the wood around in his hand. He focused as the shape in his mind emerged in the wood, and the rest of the world faded away.

John returned just as he'd finished. "You a whittler?"

William shrugged. "Used to be. Don't have much time for it now."

John looked from the turtle he'd just whittled to William and back again. "Well, you're damn good at it."

William squirmed self-consciously. "Ah, thanks. Here you go, buddy." He held out the little wooden turtle to Billy, who glanced up from his very busy work. His eyes fell on the turtle and widened.

"For me?"

"Sure."

"You made me a turtle?" Billy reached for it, holding it in his hands reverently. "John, William made me a turtle!"

"I can see that. You look after it now."

"I will! It's the best turtle I've ever seen! Can you make me a frog?"

"I don't think John wants us using up all his tools and stuff on that sort of thing."

"On the contrary, John would really like to see how you did that. Help yourself." He waved his arm expansively.

More than a little self-conscious now but figuring it would look stupid to make a fuss by refusing, William moved over to the bin of offcuts, testing a few before he found one that was the right size and weight. Then he sat down on a stool and set to work. As he worked at shaping the wood, narrowing his focus until everything else melted into the background, he was unaware of John watching him. When he'd finished, he surveyed his work. A bit rough, but no doubt the kid would be happy.

"There you go, mate," he looked up to see Billy staring at him.

"Your colors got so white," he whispered wonderingly, taking the carved frog from William and clutching it to his chest.

"That's quite a talent you've got there, son."

William shrugged as he turned his attention to John. "It's just a hobby I used to muck around with when I was a teenager."

John shrugged in return, clearly realizing the conversation was making William uncomfortable. "If you say so."

"Well, we'd better head home. Thanks for the cuppa."

"Any time."

~

*J*uniper smiled when she heard Billy's chatter as he crossed the lawn, stomped up the steps and wriggled the door handle. She'd barely opened the door when his chatter was directed at her.

"Look, Mummy! William made me a turtle AND a frog!"

"Wow!" She looked down at the wood carvings he stuffed in her hands and gasped in surprise, looking up at William. "You did this?"

"Don't you start," he replied rolling his eyes and smiling at her somewhat sheepishly. "John made a bit of a fuss," he said when she looked at him inquiringly.

"I'm not surprised. They're amazing." She ran her finger over the back of the frog then raised her eyes to his with a speculative gleam in her own.

"Anyway, are you feeling better?"

"Yes, much better, thank you. I only just got up about ten minutes ago."

"Great, because I've organized dinner." He held up a plastic shopping bag in one hand and a jaffle maker in the other.

"I thought you didn't cook?"

"I don't, but this particular meal is the dinner of champions. I wouldn't have survived university without it. You gotta try it."

"Okay." She moved aside, waving her arm, gesturing to the kitchen. "You go right ahead. I'll get Billy in the bath."

As she bathed Billy, she heard all about the day's events. He hesitated a little before telling her he and William had a fight. She was impressed with how William seemed to have handled it and as they had come back home, firm friends. It seemed to her that her son had been testing William. With bath time done and Billy playing quietly on the rug in the lounge area, Juniper moved into the kitchen.

"Hmm, interesting," she said, skeptically. He was spooning tinned spaghetti onto buttered bread, then dabbing tomato ketchup on top.

"Don't knock it til you try it."

She laughed. "Fair enough. It sounds like you guys had a pretty good day." She moved to the sink and filled a glass with water, grabbing some cold tablets on her way back behind the kitchen bench. "Billy told me he was rude to you on the beach."

William paused midway to putting a tinned spaghetti sandwich in the jaffle maker, shooting her a look that was hard to read.

"I just wanted to say, thanks for handling it the way you did. He doesn't often get like that, he's normally pretty sweet tempered. He would've been very upset if you'd gotten angry back at him."

To her surprise and confusion, she saw a look of relief flash in his eyes.

"No worries. He's a great kid." He placed three more sandwiches in the jaffle maker then closing it, leaned a hip on the bench and looked at her. "What does he mean when he talks about people's colors?" He asked quietly.

"I'm not entirely sure, but I think he means auras."

He frowned at her in confusion. "Auras?"

"They're like energy fields that people give off. They emanate from our chakras."

"You believe in that?"

"Sure, why not?"

He shrugged, clearly not really sold on the idea but then the jaffle maker sizzled, forestalling any further conversation. A flurry of activity followed as Juniper grabbed plates, glasses and a bottle of refrigerated water and moved to the little dining table. Billy clambered up onto his chair, eyeing the tray of toasted sandwiches that William placed in the center of the table with suspicion.

William picked up a sandwich and put it on Billy's plate. "Careful. It'll be a bit hot." Then he turned to Juniper, a challenge in his eye. She tentatively reached for a sandwich and placed it on her plate.

"Mmm, this is DELICIOUS!" Billy announced.

"Don't talk with your mouth full." Well, if Billy liked it, how bad could it be. She took a bite and surprised herself by finding it not too bad. It wasn't' great, but it wasn't terrible. "It's nice."

"Liar." William's eyes were brimming with amusement, and she laughed.

"It hits the spot."

"Can't ask for more than that."

"Exactly."

Once they'd finished the sandwiches and Billy had eaten some yogurt, Juniper told him it was time to brush his teeth and go to bed. He tried arguing that he wasn't tired for all of five seconds before he gave a huge yawn.

"William, can you read me my bedtime story?"

Juniper was about to interject, pretty sure William had had enough of childminding for the day, but he stopped her.

"Sure, if your Mum doesn't mind."

"I don't mind if you don't. I can squeeze in a shower."

"Let's go then."

As Juniper got ready for her shower, she couldn't help but smile at the exchange between William and Billy.

"This is my favorite book. It's about farts. Do you like farts?"

"Of course. Who doesn't?"

"Mum doesn't."

"My Mum doesn't either. Mums usually don't; They're weird like that. Don't put that there, you'll roll on it in your sleep and hurt yourself."

"But I want to cuddle it. No one's ever made me a frog before."

"Maybe just put it up here on your shelf, then you can get it first thing in the morning. How's that?"

"Okay," Billy replied, a mulish note in his voice.

"You gonna sit there looking cranky, or are we gonna read this book?"

"Read the book."

"Okay then."

After staying in her pajamas all day, feeling like she'd been run over by a truck, a shower and a change of pajamas, coupled with the cold tablets, had Juniper feeling almost well. She took advantage of the rare luxury of being able to shower without needing to listen out for Billy, taking longer than she usually would. When she got out, the house was surprisingly quiet. Surely, William hadn't left while she was in the bathroom? She stepped quietly down the short hallway to Billy's room and the sight that met her eyes melted her heart. They were both asleep, with William lying awkwardly on his side, one arm under the pillow, the other around Billy. Billy was curled against him, his palm resting flat against William's cheek in a habit familiar to Juniper. He loved to fall asleep touching her face. Well, that was just the cutest sight she'd ever seen, but she had no idea what to do now; She could hardly leave him there, but she hated to wake him. She decided to make a cup of tea and if he hadn't come out by the time she finished it, she would wake him up.

She was just putting the dinner dishes in the dishwasher when William emerged, looking mussed and gorgeous.

"Jesus, I fell asleep."

"I know."

He leaned against the bench, scrubbing his hands over his face, then into his hair.

"Cuppa?"

"Yes, please."

She turned her back to him to turn the kettle on, vibrantly aware of his gaze on her, feeling the flush of it up her spine. "So, big day, huh?"

"I wouldn't have thought so," he said with a laugh. "I didn't realize it had taken so much out of me. I really enjoyed it though. He's a really great kid."

She turned and folded her arms across her middle, smiling at him. "Thank you. It means a lot to me that you think that."

A heated silence fell between them, spinning out as they just stood there, gazing at each other. The kettle flicked off, but they remained where they were, immobile. Then William pushed away from the counter and took the two short steps to get to her. She looked up at him, her breath catching at the need in his eyes. It mirrored her own. He lowered his head and claimed her lips. She opened them, her tongue tangling with his. But this time, there was no gentle exploration, it was hot lust and it shot fire straight to her belly. He pushed his fingers into her damp hair, tilting her head to give him better access and she reveled in it, wrapping her arms around his waist, pressing against him, wanting desperately to get closer. He ran his hands down her back, cupping her bottom, pulling her harder against him, then she gasped as he lifted her up onto the bench, stepping between her knees, breaking the kiss to press hot, wet kisses down her neck. She wrapped her legs around his hips, pulling him closer until she had him where she wanted him, his erection pressed against her center.

"Jesus," he whispered huskily, finding her mouth with his own again, kissing her hungrily.

Then his hands were finding the buttons on her pajama shirt, pushing it open, his palm covering her breast, his thumb rubbing across her nipple. She moaned softly as waves of pleasure washed over her. Desperate to feel his skin, she pushed her hands under his shirt, running her palms up his back, trailing her fingers along his spine. But it wasn't enough, so she grabbed the hem of his shirt and pushed it up until he raised his arms, and she could pull it off and drop it on the floor. She curled her fingers into the hair on his chest, shivering with delight as he dropped hot, tingling kisses down her neck to her breast, then she gasped as he took her nipple in his mouth and sucked, sending a pull of pleasure to her core. She buried her fingers in his hair and let her head fall back, while he moved his lips to her other breast. She dropped her hands to his shoulders when he lifted his head and looked at her. With the tip of his finger, he traced a line from the base of her throat, down between her breasts, then lower, to the waistband of her pajama pants, running his finger slowly along the top. Once. Twice.

"You're teasing me."

A wolfish grin was his only reply as he bent his head to kiss her again, a hot, wet kiss, his tongue demanding, increasing the sweet ache between her thighs.

"William, please."

"Please, what?" He murmured.

"Please, touch me."

He pulled back and watched her as he slid his hand under the waistband of her pants, his clever fingers finding her center. He moved his hand slowly, gently, watching her all the while, the molten heat in his gaze intoxicating her. She whimpered as he rubbed against her, a low warning in the back of her mind not to be too loud; there couldn't be a worse moment for Billy to come out. She let her eyes drift closed as she took the pleasure he gave her, gripping his shoulders hard with her fingers, biting her lip as the hot pleasure washed over her. The tension built as he pushed her higher. His fingers were moving faster, more urgently, until she broke with a low moan, her body jerking against his hand, the tremors slowly subsiding as she let her head fall against his chest. She took long, deep breaths as his arms came around her, holding her close while her heart rate settled.

"We should go to bed," she said when she finally had enough breath to speak.

"Not tonight."

She lifted her head and looked at him in confusion. "You're not going to stay?"

He shook his head.

"Why not?"

"Because when we make love, I'm going to make you scream and you're not going to want to worry about waking any kids nearby."

"Oh." Well, that was hot. "But that's not very fair."

He cocked his head to one side questioningly, a smile tugging at his lips.

"One of us is happy and one of us is frustrated."

He chuckled as he bent down to retrieve his shirt. Pulling it on he said, "I'm happy and frustrated."

"But—"

He pressed a kiss to her lips. "It's fine, Juniper. I'll think of you while I'm in the shower."

"Oh." That was also hot.

He kissed her again. "I hope you're feeling better."

She eyed him quizzically. "You must know I am."

"Glad to hear it. Good night."

"Good night." She watched as he moved across the small dining area and out the front door, her body still tingling from his touch. She smiled to herself as she put the tea things away, envisioning what she would do with him the next time she had him alone.

~

"*N*ana!" The shopping bag fell from Juniper's nerveless fingers as she stopped in shock at her gate, looking down the driveway. There was a small motorhome parked at the bottom of the drive, its canopy rolled out, offering shade to her grandmother, comfortably ensconced in a lawn chair. She rose to her feet, her bright purple hair glinting in the sun as she approached her granddaughter.

"June bug!"

Juniper laughed as she threw her arms around her grandmother. "What are you doing here?"

"Rumor has it, a certain little man has a birthday coming up. As if I could miss it."

"Oh, how wonderful! But when did you get a motorhome?"

"Oh, it's not mine. It's Jasper's. When he heard I was planning a road trip, he invited himself along. I hope you don't mind, darling."

"Not at all, but who's Jasper?"

"He's my toy boy." She leaned in, her bright blue eyes twinkling merrily as she said in a conspiratorial whisper, "He's only seventy-three."

"Nana! I'm shocked! Nearly ten years your junior!"

She chuckled delightedly, then narrowed her eyes as she looked down the street. "Well, well, well. What do we have here?"

Billy was coming up the street, his hand in William's, chatting animatedly.

"Nana," Juniper said in a low, warning tone. If anything could scare a man off, it was Violet Bell's highly intrusive and inappropriate questions.

Violet turned to her, her eyes wide in innocent inquiry. "What?"

"No rude questions."

"As if I would!"

"As if you wouldn't!"

"Have you slept with him?"

"See, there you go!"

"Well, have you?"

"Not yet, but I'm going to, if you don't scare him off."

Violet sighed, the mournful note belied by the ever present twinkle in her eye. "I'll do my best, but you know, sometimes the questions just come out."

"Sure they do."

"Nana! William, look, Nana's here!" Billy let go of William's hand and ran to Violet, throwing his arms around her legs and hugging her tightly.

"Oh, my little man! Hello!"

"It's my birthday soon."

"No, is it really?"

Billy giggled. "In three sleeps! I only have to go to bed three more times, then it's my birthday! Is that why you're here?"

"Maybe. Are you going to introduce me to your friend?"

"Nana, this is my friend William. He makes frogs."

Juniper bit her lip as William stepped forward and shook her grandmother's hand. Violet Bell was a lot to take in. Five foot ten inches in her bare feet, she was dressed in a flowing purple kaftan in a paisley print, white dress pants and ballet flats. Her arms were adorned with dozens of bangles that clattered as she moved, her bright purple hair shone in the sunlight and her lips were smeared with bright red lipstick.

"William, is it?" She asked.

"Yes, ma'am."

"What are your intentions towards my granddaughter?"

William blinked and Juniper laughed. "His intentions are to come in and have lunch, which you can do too if you mind your manners."

"I always mind my manners," she replied, studiously ignoring Juniper's derisive snort.

"Do you wanna see my frog, Nana?"

"Do I ever!"

As Violet and Billy crossed the lawn and headed into the house, Juniper bent to pick up her bag before turning to William, who still seemed to be in shock. She stepped forward and kissed him on the cheek.

"Come on," she said, pulling gently on his hand.

"I, ah, think I'd better go."

"Chicken."

"Absolutely."

Juniper grinned, slipping her arm around his waist, pulling him towards the house. "You'll get used to her. She's the best."

"I don't doubt that, but I know what's going to happen. You're going to finish lunch and go back to work, which will leave me with her. Within ten minutes, she's going to know everything about me, right down to the birthmark on my left butt cheek."

"You have a birthmark on your left butt cheek?" She ran her hand down his back, giving his bottom a squeeze.

"You're not helping."

Juniper simply chuckled by way of reply, leading him up the stairs into the house.

CHAPTER 5

"*N*ow, downward dog. That's it, great job." Violet, Jasper and Billy were lined up on the grass in front of the motorhome, contorting themselves in all sorts of weird ways in the name of exercise.

Billy, his legs shaking from the effort, turned to Jasper. "Look, Jasper, I'm doing it!"

"That's the way," Jasper replied, moving smoothly into the next yoga position.

William averted his eyes as Violet pushed her bottom in the air while she turned to check Billy's posture.

She really was amazingly spry for a woman her age, but one wrong move and her shirt would be around her ears, and he definitely did not want to be caught gawking. He placed the water filter on the table Juniper indicated. She chuckled as she placed the glasses alongside. "Just be glad she's doing it with her clothes on."

"Jesus."

Juniper smiled fondly at grandmother and son.

"She means a lot to you, doesn't she?"

She turned her gaze back to him. "The world. She saved me in ways I can't even fully comprehend. Without her love and support, I'd still be languishing in Melbourne, probably unhappily married, hosting reams of society dinners and hating my life." She waved her arm in a sweeping gesture, taking in her house, the shop, the yard...him. "This is better."

"Amen to that."

She pressed a soft kiss to his lips before moving back inside to get the food platters. Leah came out from the back door of the shop, carrying an armful of plates. "Here, let me get those."

"Thanks," she said, in her quiet way.

He smiled at her reassuringly. He knew from Juniper that she was doing very well in the shop, allowing Juniper to have a day off here and there. On top of that, a few of her hand painted ceramics had sold online and Juniper was confident that with a little savvy marketing, she could push more sales, which would take a bit of pressure off the retail outlet and help both Juniper and Leah. But there was an air of vulnerability about her that made him want to constantly reassure her. He took the plates to one of the trestle tables set up along the back fence as Leah moved inside to help Juniper bring out the food.

The yoga class was over, the food and drinks were all laid out, it was time to get ready for the party.

"Come on, Billy, it's nearly party time. You need to get out of your pjs."

"Oh, but they're my favorite. They've got Bluey and Bingo on them!" He crossed his arms across his body, an angry frown, scrunching his face.

"Exactly, so you don't want to mess them up. Leah didn't give them to you so you could get sand and sauce all over them on their first day."

Seeing no reasonable come back for that logic, Billy followed Juniper inside. William sat down on the bench seat under the oak tree in the corner of the yard. It was a warm day, the air heavy and oppressive with the threat of summer rain. He tensed up when he saw Violet step out of the motorhome and make a beeline for him. She'd changed into purple slacks and a long, white, flowing shirt. Her vibrant purple hair was pulled back in a clip and she looked ready to do business. He blew out a breath of relief when he saw Mikayla, Rafe, Callum, Nora and John come through the gate and amble down the drive at just that moment, preventing the interrogation he was pretty sure Violet had planned. Billy emerged, properly dressed in shorts and a Bluey t-shirt.

"Hey! It's my birthday! Did you get me presents?"

"I sure did! What do you think this is?" Laughing, Mikayla held up the big box she was carrying, smothering Juniper's maternal protest about manners. "But I'm just going to put it over here on the gift table until your Mum says you can open it."

"Leah let me open her present first thing, when she got here," Billy protested.

"That's because Leah's not as tough as me and doesn't know how to say no." She ruffled his hair as she walked past and laid the box on the gift table, next to the one William had already put there. Nora, John, Callum and Rafe added their gifts to the

113

table, everyone laughing as Billy's eyes went wide at the sight of the big pile.

"All for me?" he asked breathlessly, looking beseechingly at his mother.

"At least let everyone get a drink and something to eat first, darling," Juniper said, moving to the food table and picking up a tray of sandwiches and offering them to the group. Once everyone settled in chairs with glasses of wine or soft drink in hand, Juniper gave Billy the go ahead.

With all the exuberance to be expected of a three old at his own birthday party, Billy ripped into the gifts, exclaiming with delight at the tonka truck Mikayla had given him, a blowup ball pit from John and Nora, a kid's ukulele from Callum and a toy ambulance from Rafe.

William admonished himself for the twinge of nerves he felt as Billy reached for the last gift on the table. He found himself moving to the back of the group as Billy ripped the wrapping off and opened the box. "Frogs!" He yelled, in absolute delight. "William gave me frogs!" He pulled one out and kissed it, making everyone laugh. Juniper leaned in and took out the little wooden pool, the lily pads delicately carved, four more frogs sitting in the bottom.

"Oh, isn't that gorgeous," Mikayla exclaimed. "Where did you get it?"

William rubbed his hand along the back of his neck, ridiculously uncomfortable. "I ah, I made it."

"No!" Her brown eyes round with surprise, she got down on her knees next to Billy and helped him set up the frogs in the pond. "Aren't you just a dark horse?"

"It's so beautiful," Juniper said softly, running her finger over a lily pad. "This is more than simple whittling, William." She raised her eyes to his, the emotion swirling in them undeniable. "How did you know how to do this?"

He shrugged. "It's just a thing I used to muck around with, when I was a kid. My family has a farm in the southern highlands and the property manager was really into carving, so he taught me."

"It's amazing."

"It's sealed, so you can put water in it."

"Can I, Mummy?" Billy asked excitedly.

"Sure."

"Mikky, can you help me?" Billy picked up the pond.

"Might be easier if you use the hose, mate. You get it and I'll turn the tap on."

As Mikayla helped Billy fill up the pond, Juniper moved to William's side. Wine glass in one hand, she draped her arm around his shoulder and with a stunning smile on her face, pulled him down and pressed a long, lush kiss against his lips.

He smiled at her when she pulled back, sliding an arm around her waist and pulling her against him. "If I'd known you were going to give me that reward, I would've given him one every day since I got here," he said, trying to lighten the moment.

"Kisses aside, you should definitely do it more often. You're very talented."

He rubbed his hand up and down her back. "Honestly, it's nothing."

"I don't agree, but it's clearly making you uncomfortable so I'll drop it. Kiss me again before I go and clean up all the wrapping paper." He kissed her, relishing the feel of her hand trailing down his arm, giving his fingers a squeeze before she moved away. Turning, he saw Violet watching him, a look of speculation in her eyes. He sighed at the inevitability of it and, grabbing a coke, moved to the bench under the oak tree. Violet soon joined him, resting her elbow on the back of the bench and turned to him, surveying him with an unreadable expression.

"You know what I sometimes think about?"

"No. What?"

"What would have happened to my girl if you hadn't stopped. Can you imagine it? Because I can, and it gives me chills. I can picture her, in pain, terrified, not knowing if the baby was going to be okay. It's a hell of a picture, let me tell you."

The thought gave him chills, too.

"When I imagine that picture, I dismiss it, and I replace it with what really was. That she had someone with her, someone who held her, encouraged her, helped her. I can't tell you how that makes me feel, William, because I don't have the words for it. So, all I can say is, thank you."

William nodded, unable to speak past the lump in his throat. Violet let the silence play out for a little while, then she said, "Has she told you about her family?"

"A little."

Violet sighed. "I blame myself, you know. I lost the love of my life when my son was only nine years old. God, I was so heartbroken when Henry died. I went a little crazy, I won't lie to you. He'd left me well off financially, so I just checked out of life. I took Michael around the world, trekking through South America, ashrams in India, abbeys in Europe, all of it. I just wanted to live, you know, for Henry, because if he taught me nothing else, he taught me that you have to live your best life. It's short and it could be over like that," she clicked her fingers. "So now I wonder if I made Michael feel insecure." She sighed. "Or maybe he's a changeling because I can't believe that any son of mine could be so cold, so avaricious, so superficial as to discard someone like Juniper. Because that's what he did, you know. He married a woman with a heart colder than a dead fish. Then they had a little bitch of a daughter, just as cold as them. But then, the shock of all shocks, they had Juniper, all golden curls and green eyes and joy." She paused and William followed her gaze to where Juniper was kneeling on the grass with Billy, laughing as he splashed the frogs in the pond. "I knew from the moment I saw her she would be mine more than theirs. So, I paid Michael one hundred thousand dollars for the joy of naming her. Can you imagine that? Taking money for something like that?" She laughed derisively. "But he would have called her something plain and dull and I wouldn't have it." She paused again, looking down at her hands, clasped tightly in her lap. "I did my best for her, but she was like a shrinking violet there. It warms my heart to see the life she's made for herself here. It was hard won, and it cost her a lot." The sad note in her voice suddenly changed, becoming more upbeat, lighter. "But she's gained a lot. That baby of hers was sent by angels. I'm sure of it." She smiled as she watched Billy, shrieking with laughter, fall back on the grass as Juniper splashed him. "What about you, William? Are you living your best life?"

The sudden change of tack startled him, which he was sure was her intention. But she'd shared a lot with him in the last few minutes and although his instinct was to deflect, he felt it was only fair to give her question serious consideration. Was he living his best life? "I don't know."

She snorted. "Then you're deceiving yourself."

Maybe he was. He'd definitely felt, over the last few years, like he'd lost his place. Lost the certainty he'd felt about his life. The restlessness that had plagued him churned at his guts, a constant reminder that no, he hadn't been living his best life, if only he were brave enough to acknowledge it. When he thought about it, he realized that the churning feeling had lessened recently. To the point that sometimes he didn't even feel it at all. He shied away from that idea, merely responding to Violet with a shrug, "Maybe I'm not." It was irrelevant anyway. What could he do to change his life? He certainly couldn't abandon his parents and their life's work. There was no possible way either of them could run the business without him, and he wouldn't see them lose it because he wanted to be selfish. It was duty and love that bound him and there was no escaping that.

"You can't fix what you don't acknowledge." She pushed to her feet, surprising him by leaning over and pressing a kiss on his forehead. "She won't live in Sydney. She couldn't do it. Even for you." She moved away to take a seat next to Nora.

He felt a little thunderstruck as Juniper approached him. "Everything okay?" She sat down next to him, snuggling in when he put his arm around her shoulders.

"Sure. I managed not to tell her about my birthmark."

Juniper laughed. "She got you thinking?"

"Yep."

"She does that. It's her super-power. In my experience, you're usually better off than before she got you going, if that helps."

He wasn't sure it did, but he was saved from replying by Billy walking over, the wooden frogs nestled in his shirt, which he'd folded at the front to hold them. He clambered into William's lap and proceeded to lay all the frogs out, sharing their name and ages, their favorite foods and colors.

~

A few evenings later, Juniper stepped out of Billy's room, making her way to the kitchen just as Violet came in from the motorhome.

"You probably don't want to do that," Violet said.

"Huh? You don't want a cuppa?"

"I do, but you don't."

"Ah, yes I do." Juniper turned to look at Violet questioningly.

"Your man's home. He got back about ten minutes ago, I would say."

"What, how do you know that? Psychic flash?"

Violet gave a rich, deep chuckle. "No, darling. Jasper and I just took a walk down the street and saw a light come on up there."

Juniper stood stock still in the kitchen for a long moment before whirling into action. She hurried, packing two shopping bags, then scurried to her bedroom to pack an overnight bag.

Shopping bags in hand, overnight bag slung over her shoulder, she paused long enough to kiss Violet on the cheek before moving towards the door. "I'll see you tomorrow. I love you."

"I love you too, June Bug. Have lots of orgasms!"

Juniper chuckled. "I will!"

The three-minute drive up to the lighthouse had never felt so long to Juniper but she was finally knocking on the door to the little house next to the lighthouse, her heart thudding in antici- pation. Then the door was swinging wide, and William was there, backlit by the wash of light from a single lamp in the lounge room.

"Hey."

"Hey, yourself." The pleasure in his eyes at the sight of her warmed her blood.

"Have you eaten?"

"I was just about to make a spaghetti jaffle."

"Thank the stars, I arrived just in the nick of time." She stepped inside, pressing a kiss to his lips but evading his arms and sliding past him. She slipped her sandals off and dumped her overnight bag next to them, by the wall. She took the shopping bags into the kitchen, heaving them onto the bench just as William switched the light on. She started unpacking the bags, removing a saucepan, wooden spoon, pasta, homemade basil pesto, pine nuts, and parmesan cheese. "You can set the table," she said, handing him two ceramic candlestick holders and the accompa- nying candles. As he took them from her, he leaned in to try and kiss her, but she just smiled and pushed at him. "The table. And I'd love a glass of wine." She filled the saucepan with water and placed it on the stovetop, and then turned the dial up to high. "Good business trip?"

He was still wearing suit pants and his business shirt, unbut- toned at the collar and the tie discarded. His hair looked disheveled, like he'd been running his fingers through it. He shrugged as he handed her a glass of chilled white wine. He'd traveled down to Melbourne to scout out a location in the Dandenong Ranges for a corporate retreat. He'd been gone three days and God, she'd missed him. But he didn't look happy, his shrug indicating something was up. "Mum and Dad are happy. The building is perfect for a retreat, the price is right, it needs some work so we can add value." He shrugged again.

"What is it?"

"Nothing." She tilted her head to one side, looking at him for a long moment but he had that shuttered expression on his face that he sometimes got, so she didn't push it. Turning away, she put her wine glass down and opened the packet of fresh pasta, tipping it into the boiling water. He came up behind her and wrapped his arms around her waist. He then pressed a kiss to the side of her neck. "I'm sorry."

She turned into his arms, brushing her lips lightly across his. "You don't have anything to apologize for." In a weary gesture, he dropped his forehead to hers so she just stood there. She wrapped her arms around his waist, offering what comfort she could for whatever was bothering him. After a little while, he leaned back and looked down at her, the slow heating in his eyes unmistakable. He moved to lower his head, but she stopped him, pressing her fingertips to his lips. "Set the table."

"Such a slave driver," he said with a long-suffering sigh as he pulled away, making her chuckle.

By the time the pasta was cooked, Juniper was mixing in the pesto and parmesan, William had the table set and the candles lit.

"Lovely," she said, bringing the bowl of pasta and her glass of wine over. "Now, it's no spaghetti toastie, but I think you'll like it," she said as they sat down.

"I'll do my best," he replied, giving her a mischievous grin. "So, what have you been up to while I've been away?" He asked, topping up her wine glass.

"Oh, I took Billy, Nana and Jasper to the butterfly enclosure. That big blue butterfly sure does love the Bells, she couldn't get enough of Billy. She followed him around, landed on his head and wouldn't' get off. He loved it at first but by the time we got to the exit, he was sick of it. You should have seen his expression when she landed on his nose. Cross eyed and cross at the same time. I'll have to show you the photos."

He laughed appreciatively and she thought she was going some way to alleviating his mood. "This is amazing," he said, twirling more pasta around his fork.

"Better than a toastie?"

He held up his finger and thumb, a small distance apart. "By about this much."

"Cheeky."

When their bowls were empty, Juniper leaned forward in her chair, resting her chin on her hand and wrapping her fingers around the stem of her wine glass. William leaned back in his chair, one hand in his pocket, the other holding his glass. She took a sip of wine, pleased with the way his eyes watched her every move.

"You've come here with a plan, tonight."

"I have."

He quirked an inquiring brow.

"The way I see it, the night's going to go one of two ways."

"Hmm?"

"Option one, you're going to take me to bed, where we make slow, passionate love all night long." Her skin warmed as the heat swirled in his eyes.

"I see. And option two?"

She waited a beat, before saying, "We don't make it to the bedroom, and you take me hard up against the wall." She sipped her wine, feeling a tug of desire in her core. She watched as he rose to his feet, never taking her eyes off him as he came around to her side of the table and taking her hand, pulled her to her feet.

"I'm taking option one," he said, causing her to gasp as he swept her up in his arms.

"Hmm, a wise choice," she replied sagely, wrapping her arms around his neck and nibbling on his ear.

"You'd better stop doing that, or we'll quickly move to option two," he said as he crossed the small lounge room, into his bedroom.

She stopped. Option one really did sound amazing. She kept her arms around his neck as he put her down on the floor next to the bed. She pulled him closer, pressing herself against him, finding his mouth with hers.

"I have to tell you something," she whispered against his lips.

"Mm?" He lifted his head to look down at her.

"I've organized birth control."

"You have?"

"Mm hmm. I did it the day after the music festival."

He smiled. "You knew I was a sure thing, then."

She smiled back. "I knew I wanted you. Here. Like this." She found his mouth again, sliding her tongue over his bottom lip, nipping gently with her teeth. He moved his hands from her waist down to her hips, pulling her against him. She sighed as he opened his mouth and she slid her tongue across his, the taste of him was intoxicating. She'd wanted this for what felt like an eternity and so the need was there, pushing at her. She felt the swirling heat and reminded herself to slow down. All the little touches, the kisses, that night in her kitchen, all leading to this moment. Now they had all night and she wanted to make the most of it.

He moved his hands to her bottom, cupping her against him. She felt his need for her, felt his erection and it only inflamed her more. She kissed him more urgently, running her hands down his chest, pulling the hem of his shirt up, desperate to get her hands on his skin. God, she just wanted to rip his shirt open, run her fingers through the hair on his chest, lick him. Everywhere.

He smiled against her lips. "Honey, slow down."

"Can't." She reached for the buttons on his shirt with shaking fingers, fumbling with them. He brought his hands up and covered hers, holding them still against his heart. She looked up at him, noting the heat mixed with amusement in his eyes. And something else. Something she couldn't name. He pulled her hands away and unbuttoned his shirt. As soon as he'd undone the last one, she ran her palms up his chest. She pushed the shirt off his shoulders, pressing hot kisses along his neck, his collar bone, and down his chest. The heat was like a fever, flashing through her system before it settled as a dull ache between her legs.

She kissed him again, that delicious tangling of tongues. She felt his hands at the zipper of her dress, the whisper as he lowered it with agonizing slowness, the caress of his fingertips up her spine before he reached her shoulders and grabbing the top of the dress, pulled it down until the sleeves were just above her elbows. Then he tightened his grip at the back, so that she couldn't move her arms, kissing her all the while. His kisses were deep and drugging. He trailed soft, wet kisses down her neck, dipping his tongue in the groove at the base of her throat where her pulse throbbed, then lower, to her breast. He turned his body and shifted backwards until he reached the bed, sitting down and pulling her between his knees. He still had her arms trapped and the urge to touch him caused her palms to itch.

"William." She was begging and he knew it. He released her dress, and she hastily pulled her arms from the sleeves, burying her fingers in his hair, pulling his head back and laying her mouth across his as his arms wrapped around her. But he was having none of it, breaking away to kiss her breasts through the blue lace of her bra. She gasped as he covered her nipple with his mouth. The tug of his lips sent a pulsating ache to her core, and she gasped again. It was quickly becoming too much—more than she could bear. He loosened his hold, running his hands over her bottom and lower, down the back of her thighs until he found the hem of her dress, then sliding under to caress the backs of her knees. She'd had no idea that was an erogenous zone, but she almost buckled as he ran the tips of his fingers down to the top of her shins. He continued to run them up and over the backs of her thighs, then over her bottom where he gripped the top of her underwear and pulled. He broke the kiss to look up at her as he lowered her underwear to the floor and she stepped out of them, then he traced that same path back up her legs, pausing at the sensitive place behind her knees, bringing his hands around to the front, caressing her legs, pushing her dress up, leaning forward to press hot kisses to her thighs. God, she wanted...needed more. But he continued to tease her, running his fingers through the damp curls at the juncture of her thighs then moving away.

She whimpered with frustration. "You're tormenting me."

He smiled up at her, his eyes dark, fathomless, like aged brandy. "A little." Then watching her all the while, he slipped one finger between her legs, and she moaned, biting her lip. "You can scream." She moaned again, digging her fingers into his shoulders. She could barely stand up. With one hand busy between her legs, he wrapped his other arm around her hips, holding her upright. Feeling steadier, she surrendered to the rhythm of his fingers inside her, his clever, sensitive fingers. Her breathing becoming more ragged, she moaned again, letting her head fall back, feeling the pleasure build, the tension winding tighter and tighter until she snapped, crying out as the orgasm rippled through her, her hips jerking against him. "Jesus," she said on a ragged breath as she wrapped her arms around him, resting her cheek on the top of his head as the last of the tremors passed through her. His arms came around her waist, holding her close.

"Your heart's pounding," he said, after a while.

"I'm not surprised." She straightened up, moving her fingers to toy with the hair at the nape of his neck. "It's cheeky how you do that."

"Do what?" he asked innocently.

She gave a derisive snort. "You know exactly what. Get me going so I can't think of anything else, until it's all about me and not about you."

His lips curved in a soft smile.

"Well, two can play at that game." She leaned down and kissed him, just a slight brushing of her lips over his. Soft. Delicate. Then she stepped back, reaching to undo the clip on her bra, pulling it down her arms and dropping it to the floor. The dress soon followed. His gaze roved over her naked body hungrily and she felt the little flicker of heat start all over again. He reached out and wrapped his fingers around her wrist, pulling her forward, but she pulled away, shaking her head at him. With her eyes never leaving his, she sank to her knees in front of him. She then ran her hands up his thighs, brushing ever so lightly over the bulge between his legs, to his belt buckle. She watched him as she slowly undid it, then the button and zip on his pants. He was gritting his teeth, the muscles in his jaw bunching. She slid her hand along the length of him, shuffling forward before leaning in and slowly running her tongue around the tip of his cock. She felt the tremor move through him, so she did it again. Then she lifted her gaze again, not blinking as she took him inside her mouth. She felt his effort to keep a tight rein on his control. She closed her eyes then, giving herself over to the pleasure of pleasuring him, relishing the feel of his hands in her hair, the sound of his shuddering breath as she moved on him, licking and sucking, running her hand up and down his length. It was deeply arousing for her, his response inflaming her.

"Juniper, stop."

She felt he was close to the brink and although she wanted him hot for her, she also wanted him inside her. She got to her feet, only for his arm to wrap around her waist. He pulled her down on the bed where he covered her body with his own, his lips claiming hers in a searing kiss. Need shot through her, lighting her ablaze as his hand found her breast, squeezing, his thumb rubbing across her nipple. She pushed his pants down further until he wriggled them off and they were both, finally, naked. She wrapped her legs around his hips, wanting him to fill the emptiness, and ease the desire. He positioned himself, then with aching, agonizing slowness, he was pushing into her. She arched against him as he pulled out, then pushed back in with that long, slow thrust. Then again. And again.

"Kiss me."

She pulled his head down and with her eyes still closed, found his lips and kissed him for all she was worth. She ran her hands down his back, to his hips, digging her fingers in, willing him to go harder, faster. He did, thrusting his hips, his breath hot against her neck, the sound of flesh slapping against flesh. She moaned, then moaned again. He reached an arm under her hips and tilted her up, changing the angle, hitting her exactly where she needed it most and she was lost. Crying out, she felt wave after wave of pleasure pulse through her until she reached glorious release. She felt his body, taut against her as he came, then the hot rush of him filling her as the final tremors of her orgasm rippled through her. She lay under the weight of him, her legs still around his hips, her hands tracing lazy circles up and down his back.

He lifted his head to press soft kisses up her neck, along her jawline to her lips. She sighed at the sheer loveliness of it. He shifted then, so she tightened her legs around him, wanting him to stay just where he was. He chuckled, saying, "I can't stay here forever."

"I don't see why not."

But he rolled off her, keeping his arm under her so she went with him, then she was curled against his side, her head on his shoulder. Not a bad compromise. She laid her hand over his heart, feeling the strong beat under her palm. His fingers trailed lightly along her hip in a gentle caress.

"Oh, I forgot."

"What?"

"I brought dessert." She lifted her head to look at him, lying back on the pillow with his eyes closed.

"Yeah? What'd you bring?"

"Banana splits with ice cream and chocolate sauce."

He opened one eye to look at her askance. "You think you're going to introduce chocolate sauce to this equation without it being requisitioned for naughtier purposes?"

She looked at him for a long moment, her eyes wide. "Good point. I'll just go and get it."

CHAPTER 6

he sun rose over the Tasman Sea slowly, gently, a soft
ball of light just creeping over the horizon. But when
she got there, she sent her light streaking across the waves,
through the window in the little cottage by the lighthouse,
hitting William full in the face. He'd forgotten to close the block
out blinds the night before and boy, was he paying for it now.
He rubbed his hand over his face and opened his eyes, squinting
in the flooding light. He heard Juniper sigh next to him and
turned to look at her. She shifted in her sleep, trying to evade
the creep of sunshine. He got up and padded to the blinds,
quietly lowering one just enough to stop the rays from hitting
the bed. It didn't shut out all the light, but it would be enough
that she could keep sleeping. His heart squeezed painfully in his
chest as he looked at her. Sleeping Beauty. Such a cliché. But
she was just so stunningly beautiful that it almost hurt to look at
her. And here she was, in his bed. Finally. She was a revelation;
a generous lover who gave as good as she got. But she was also
fun; the thing with the chocolate sauce making them both laugh
and feel turned on at the same time. He felt his body stirring at
the memories and backed away from the bed. He could let her

sleep a little longer, feeling pretty confident that when she did wake up, there was more fun to be had.

He was just finishing stacking the previous night's dinner dishes in the dishwasher when he heard movement from the bedroom, then Juniper calling out, "I'm just going to have a shower."

"Okay. There are towels in the cupboard in the hallway near the bedroom door."

"I've got chocolate sauce in my hair," she said, coming out of the bedroom, holding a towel and a bag of toiletries.

"Not even sorry," he replied, grinning at her.

"Me either."

He watched her as she turned back into the hallway, her exceptionally fine ass as she walked away a treat for his eyes.

She came out twenty minutes later in a terry toweling robe that finished at the knees and her hair wrapped up in a purple hair towel. "I'm making breakfast and then I'm going home to give Nana a break."

"Sounds good. Can I do anything?"

"You can make the coffee."

"Already done." He followed her into the little kitchenette and pointed to the steaming mug of coffee on the bench.

"Oh, amazing." She picked it up and took a sip, her eyes closing blissfully.

He grabbed his mug and moved to the entrance to the kitchenette to watch her. She moved about with ease, pulling ingredients out of his fridge he hadn't even noticed her put there the night before—

eggs, mushrooms, shallots, cheese, capsicum, and herbs. Then she stopped, frowning, riffling through the shopping bag she'd brought. She sighed with frustration. "Have you got an egg whisk?"

"Ah, no, probably not. I've only got the basics."

She rolled her eyes at him. "An egg whisk is basic."

"Well, you know, I've just set it up minimally for now. The caretaker will have a budget to set it up how they want when the time comes."

His words dropped like a bomb in the little kitchen, a sudden and harsh reminder that his staying there was temporary. It had grabbed him by the throat the night before, when he'd returned from Melbourne. The gut-wrenching restlessness had returned anew, leaving him feeling confused and empty. Then she had turned up, her smile was soft but her green eyes were hot for him. So, he'd let it go for the moment, just buried himself in her and let it go.

She responded by ignoring his statement, just reaching into the top drawer and grabbing a fork. "This'll do."

He wanted to say something, to acknowledge how he was feeling, how she might be feeling, but he had no idea what to say so he left it.

"You can make some toast, if you like." She glanced up at him, a strained smile on her face.

"Sure."

He dropped the bread into the toaster. She diced the vegetables and set them aside, dropped a dab of butter in a frying pan she'd brought with her, added the egg, sipped her coffee, and stirred the egg in the pan. The tension grew until he could almost feel it pressing against him.

"Look—"

She turned to him abruptly, urgency in her eyes. "Let's not talk about it. Let's not think about it. Let's just enjoy it for what is, right now, in this moment. I don't want to think about tomorrow."

"Okay." He reached out, wrapped his fingers around her wrist and pulled her to him. With his other hand he tilted her chin up, pressing a soft, gentle kiss on her lips. The toast popped, startling them both, breaking the moment. She laughed. It sounded almost natural.

They ate scrambled eggs on toast out on the little paved area in front of the sliding doors, keeping it light.

"You'll have to bring Billy up."

"Definitely. He'd love the lighthouse."

He thought about it for a little while. "I could have a barbecue."

"You don't own a barbecue," she teased.

"I'll get one. Do you think Mikky and Rafe would come?"

"Yeah, definitely. John and Nora, too, if you like. Which of course means Callum. Then it would be weird not to invite Leah. After that, you may as well invite the whole town."

He laughed. "I'll start by ordering the barbecue."

"Good plan."

They finished breakfast and made quick work of cleaning the kitchen.

"I'd better get dressed." Juniper moved out of the kitchen, heading towards the hallway.

William was right behind her though, wrapping his arm around her waist and pulling her back against him, pressing hot kisses down the side of her neck. "In a minute." He spun her around, delighting in the fire that was already flaring in her eyes. He put his hands on her hips, pulling her hard against him, claiming her lips in a searing kiss. He walked her backwards until she was up against the lounge room wall, satisfied by her gasp of shock. She was returning his kiss with fervor, her tongue tangling with his, her fingers buried in his hair. "I'm taking option two."

"Mm, excellent." She reached up and pulled the towel from her hair, dropping it to the floor, wrapping her arms tight around his neck. He let the kiss spin out, hot and wet. He just needed to get his hands on her. Without breaking the kiss, he reached for the tie of her robe, untying it and pushing it open. He slid his hands up over her breasts, her nipples pebbling against his palms, her whimper of pleasure turning him on even more. He hungered for her and he wanted to know she felt the same. He wanted her drenched. He slid one hand down over her waist, down her hip, continuing down her thigh. He then pulled her leg up, hooking it over his hip, grinding his erection against her center. His shorts were the only thing that stopped him from entering her as she groaned with pleasure, pushing herself against him. He broke off the kiss, grazing his teeth along her jawline and down her neck. Then, in one smooth movement, he sank to his knees, shifting her leg so that it was draped over his shoulder. She was right there, open for him. He pressed hot, hungry kisses along the inside of her thigh, to her core.

"Oh, god," she whispered as he ran his tongue over her. Her scent surrounded him. He felt drunk on the taste of her as he flicked his tongue against her clitoris. She cried out, moving herself against his mouth and he could feel the tension building in her. "Stop," she said huskily. He didn't want to, he wanted to push her until she fell over the edge and broke into a thousand pieces. "William, stop." He pulled back and looked up at her, her eyes dark emerald green and drowsy as they met his. God, she was so beautiful it almost made him want to cry. She pulled on his shoulder, willing him to his feet. "Inside me," she said urgently, tearing at his shirt as he stood up, forcing it over his head. He hurriedly pushed his shorts down and sliding his hands down to her buttocks. He lifted her, pressing her against the wall as her legs wrapped around his waist, her arms around his neck. He thrust into her, almost coming undone immediately. She was so hot and wet. He thrust again and she cried out, "Harder." He thrust harder, again. Again. Again. One more long, hard thrust and she went over, her fingers digging into his shoulders as she screamed. Her body tightening around him, sent him over with her and he let himself go, pumping into her until he came. Her head fell forward on his shoulder as she let out a sobbing breath and he could feel her heart hammering against his. She shivered with pleasure as the last convulsions of her orgasm moved through her. He held her there for a long time, trying to get his breath back and give his heart rate a chance to steady. "Okay, I'm quite a fan of option two."

He chuckled. "Me too."

～

"I want details."

"Well, you're not getting them, you pervert." Juniper reached for a chip, dipping it in aioli and grinning at Mikayla. Lunch with her girlfriends, the bustle of the café, the late summer sunshine, an evening and morning of hot sex, left her feeling pretty good.

"Some friend you are. Just tell me one thing."

"Mm?"

"Was it good?"

Juniper sighed.

"Fuck off."

Juniper chuckled.

"How many times did he make you come?"

She counted out on her fingers, Mikayla's eyes widening comically when she lifted her other hand.

"Well, good on you." She reached across the table, rubbing Juniper's arm. "I'm super happy for you."

"Thanks."

Leah cleared her throat and they both turned to her. "Is it...is it really that good?"

They looked at her a little non-plussed, not sure how to answer.

"It can be. With the right person," Mikayla answered quietly.

"Oh, right." She looked down at her coffee cup, stirring the spoon absently. Then she sighed and looked up at them. There was a deep sadness in her eyes that broke Juniper's heart. "Maybe I've been unlucky, then."

"Did you never...with your husband?" Mikayla's eyes were full of concerned sympathy.

She shook her head. "He, ah, he didn't really find me attractive."

Alarm bells went off in Juniper's head as Mikayla burst out with "What the fuck?"

Leah shrugged dismissively. "Well, you know, I'm not very tall, or curvy, or...blonde."

"No, fuck that. Firstly, you're gorgeous. Secondly, you don't marry someone and then tell them they're not absolutely gorgeous every second of the day. Unless you're a giant, stonking arse."

"Amen to that," Juniper corroborated.

Leah looked at them thoughtfully. "Right. So, maybe he was just a giant, stonking arse."

"I don't think there's much maybe about it. How long did you say you were married for?"

"Nine years."

Mikayla gasped. "Nine years of marriage and he never made you come?"

Leah shrugged uncertainly. "I think it's me."

Mikayla snorted. "Unlikely." She tilted her head to one side, surveying Leah for a long moment. "Have you ever...you know... on your own?"

Leah blushed. "No."

"Hmm, well—"

Juniper, seeing that Leah was starting to get really uncomfortable, shot Mikayla a look. "Hey, would you look at the time? Leah, I think it's time we headed back."

"Okay," Leah replied, barely disguising her relief. "I'll get back and make a start on setting up that new display we talked about."

"Great, thank you."

With a shy smile for both of them, Leah pulled her bag over her shoulder and strode off up Main Street. After making sure she was out of earshot, Juniper turned to Mikayla. "Jesus, her ex sounds like a massive dickhead."

"He sure does," Mikayla replied, tapping her forefinger thoughtfully to her lips.

"Oh god, you're trying to think who you can set her up with."

"I sure am. It would have to be someone very patient and kind, who really knows what he's doing." Her eyes lit up. "Callum!"

"I don't think that's a great idea."

"What? Why not?"

"I don't know, I just think she's quite uncomfortable around him. Haven't you noticed?"

Mikayla frowned. "Not particularly. She's always quiet, so it's hard to tell."

Juniper rose to her feet. "I think we're best off leaving it for now. We just have to make sure she knows we're here if she wants to talk about anything."

"Yeah, maybe you're right," Mikayla said doubtfully, as she stood up, leaving her share of the tab on the table. Juniper smiled at her. She was always and forever action oriented, especially when it came to people she cared about. She hated to see anyone struggling and would always go out of her way to help if she could.

"I am right," Juniper said with a smile as they walked down the street.

"Okay. But I'm gonna keep an eye on her."

"Me too."

∾

"Seriously, mate, it sucks to be you."

William laughed at Mikayla. "It's not bad, is it?"

As their final stop in the tour of the compound, William, Juniper, Billy, Mikayla, Rafe, Callum, Leah, Nora, John, Violet and Jasper were all squished into the top of the lighthouse, gazing out at the turbulent sea. Thick clouds hovered, creating an oppressive atmosphere that begged for the relief of rain. William just had to hope it held off long enough for the barbecue. Once he'd mentioned the idea of hosting a barbecue, almost as a joke, to Juniper, he'd realized how much he would enjoy it. Never one to muck around once he'd decided on something, he'd gone online and ordered a grand, stainless steel six burner monstrosity that had arrived within forty-eight hours. Feeling a little odd, he'd casually mentioned it to John, relieved that he'd jumped on the idea with enthusiasm. Once the invitation had been passed on to Nora, it was a done deal with snacks, salads and desserts organized amongst the group. With a BYO chair policy instituted by Juniper and a table made of sawhorses and long lengths of unstained flooring, all that was left for him to do was order the meat.

"I'm going to head back down and get the barbecue on."
William squeezed through the group and down the spiral stairs,
smiling to himself when he heard Juniper's footsteps behind
him. He moved through the door, turning quickly to grab her as
she came through, pressing her up against the warm sandstone
wall of the lighthouse. "We didn't get to say a proper hello."
She'd arrived with Billy, Violet and Jasper so all he'd been
allowed was a chaste peck on the cheek. She smiled, understanding exactly what he meant, before wrapping her arms
around his neck and laying her lips across his in a passionate
kiss. Their tongues entwined and he felt the hot stirrings of lust,
pushing her hard against the wall as she buried her fingers in his
hair. He heard the stomping of multiple pairs of feet on the iron
staircase and pulled back abruptly, seeing his regret mirrored in
her eyes. "God, I can't get enough."

"Me either." She linked her fingers in his as they walked to the
little cottage and through the sliding doors to the kitchen.
"Maybe I could come back tonight after Billy goes to bed. I'm
sure Nana won't mind, but I'd want to be back home before he
wakes in the morning."

"Okay." He pulled the meat out of the fridge, smiling at her
when she took it from him, and he followed her back out to the
patio.

"Nana's probably going to head back to Byron Bay soon, so we
have to make the most of it."

He sighed as he turned the barbecue on. He wanted to ask what
would happen after Violet left but as they stepped out, the rest
of the group was ambling across the lawn from the lighthouse.

"Jeez, mate, you sure know how to buy a barbie." Callum grabbed three beers from the ice box, handing one each to Rafe and William before taking the seat Rafe folded out for him.

William laughed at Callum, looking at the giant barbecue. "Yeah, I might have gone a bit overboard." He waved his hand over the hotplate, judging if it was hot enough and started throwing the sausages and meat patties on, getting a kick of satisfaction as they instantly sizzled and in no time at all, the mouthwatering scent was wafting on the air.

John approached the barbecue, a harried, flushed look on his face. "Jesus Christ, give me a beer."

Concerned, Callum reached into the icebox nestled against the window and pulled out a bottle, handing it to his father. "What is it?"

"Violet's talking to your mother."

William and Callum glanced over, seeing Nora and Violet in their fold out chairs facing the sea, heads bent close, engaged in an intense conversation. Jasper was alongside them, leaning back contentedly, his gray hair blowing softly in the breeze. The chair John had been sitting on was knocked over on the grass. "So?"

"Well, it's Violet. What do you think they're talking about?" William had a few ideas, but Callum shrugged, bewildered. He obviously hadn't had much experience with Violet. "They're talking about sex."

"Oh," Callum shifted his shoulders uncomfortably.

"Tantric sex."

"Ooh,"

"Which means I'm going to have to—"

"Okay, Dad, I get the picture," Callum interrupted hastily. His attention was diverted by Mikayla, coming back from the car with a music dock under her arm. She plugged it into an external outlet just near where they were sitting, blue toothed her cell phone to it, then watching her brother carefully, pressed play. Callum swore at her as the first strains of a One Direction hit split the air.

She grinned mischievously. "Just jokes." She quickly flicked through her phone, found her seventies playlist and pressing play, slapped Callum on the back as she grabbed a beer from the icebox and moved away to her seat next to Juniper and Leah. William found their byplay hugely entertaining but felt a frisson of alarm as Mikayla bent her head to Juniper's and they quickly engaged in an intense conversation, shooting him glances every now and then.

"They're talking about you, you know." Rafe gestured with his beer bottle.

"I'm aware." William looked away, turning the sausages absently. He could only imagine what they were saying. Leah, for her part, seemed to be more focused on playing with Billy as he sat in her lap than listening to the conversation. He was grateful for that small mercy, at least. Then he saw Juniper nod enthusiastically and look over at him, a beatific smile lighting up her face. Well, it wasn't terrible, whatever it was, he thought as his heart thumped hard against his ribs and he smiled back at her.

He flipped the burger patties, listening idly as the conversation around him turned to the upcoming football season, surprised to find that they were all Sydney Swans fans. Usually, when he traveled south of the border, he was the odd one out, since most Victorians barracked for one of the local teams.

"I think this might be Franklin's last season." John leaned back further in the chair, taking a swig of beer.

"Yeah, you might be right. Not sure who's around to step up once he's gone," Callum said thoughtfully.

John chuckled. "We'll be right for this season at least. I reckon we're looking the goods for a finals berth."

"Cheers to that." Rafe leaned over and clinked his beer bottle against John's.

"If we do get in, you guys should come up to Sydney for a game. We've got a corporate box at the SCG."

As one, John, Callum and Rafe turned to stare at him then John's face split into a wide grin. "I'll hold you to that offer, son."

William laughed. "See that you do." He switched the barbecue off and moved the sausages and patties onto a wide tray, taking it over to the makeshift table. "Lunch is up," he called, stepping back as everyone came over, grabbing plates, napkins and cutlery before descending on the table. The flow of chatter never stopped as they all piled their plates with bread rolls, garden salad, potato salad, sausages and meat patties and settled into an informal circle to eat their lunch. It was all just so easy and relaxed, such a far cry from the types of gatherings his parents arranged. They were usually formally catered and nearly always used for networking. You'd never see anyone take something from someone else's plate, like Mikayla was just now doing to Rafe, or a toddler having a minor meltdown because his mother demanded that he eat something green, like Billy was doing, or someone eating lunch while sitting in their lover's lap, like Violet was doing with Jasper. There certainly wouldn't have been any Led Zeppelin blaring. Observing it all, William recognized that he loved every second of it.

"Is there something wrong with this meat?" Mikayla asked loudly.

William started. "I don't think so, why?"

"You're the only one not eating it."

"Oh, right." He piled up a plate and took the empty chair next to Juniper.

"All good?" She asked, rubbing his arm.

"Yep," he replied with a smile.

She looked at him for a long moment, then seemingly satisfied with what she saw, turned back to make sure Billy was eating his lunch.

Once lunch was finished, Mikayla leaned back in her chair, stretched her arms above her head and declared, "I'm stuffed."

"Me too," Nora said. "I could have a nap right now."

"No time for that, Mum! We gotta work off lunch."

Rafe groaned. "You're joking."

She slapped him on the thigh. "This is hardly a joking matter." Then she jumped to her feet and strode off around the edge of the cottage.

"She's not serious?" Callum sighed.

William looked at Juniper inquiringly, but she just shrugged. She didn't know what was going on either. William was even more mystified when Nora and John picked up their chairs and walked off. John paused, before rounding the corner of the cottage. "Violet, Jasper. You'll want to bring your chairs."

More than curious, everyone rose to their feet and followed. William laughed when he saw Mikayla stepping away from her car with a football under her arm.

"I'm the first captain. I pick William. Rafe, who you got?"

"Why does Rafe get to be captain?" Callum protested.

"Oh, okay then. Leah, you can be captain. Who you got?"

"No way! Leave me out of it," Leah replied with a quiet laugh.

"Okay, you can be goal umpire, then. Go with Dad, he'll set you up. Juniper, you can be umpire at the other end. Unless you wanna play?"

John had gone into the Keeper's cottage and emerged with four traffic cones, moving about the large clearing between the buildings to lay them out at either end. "Not on your life," Juniper replied, walking over to where he was placing the traffic cones in position.

"So that leaves me and William on one team, Rafe and Callum on the other. You guys can sort out who's captain amongst yourselves. Billy's with me."

"Huh? Why do you get Billy?"

"Coz I called dibs on him." Mikayla rolled her eyes at her brother.

"No, you didn't."

"Yes, I did."

"You didn't. You just said, Billy's with me. That's not calling dibs."

William turned to Rafe. "Are they always like this?"

Rafe laughed. "Always. The Sinclairs take their sport very seriously."

Billy, listening to the exchange avidly, grinned from ear to ear, when they both turned to him and Mikayla said, "It's up to you, my man. Whose team you wanna be on?"

Without hesitating, he moved over to William, slipping his hand in his. Mikayla clapped delightedly. "Okay, coz we scored Billy, you can choose which end you wanna kick to first."

"Big of you," Callum observed. "We'll take the lodge end. Unless Rafe objects?"

"Nah, all good."

"Great, let's go. Dad!" Mikayla handballed the ball to John, who caught it adeptly and moved to the center of the clearing.

William looked around. God, this was hilarious. Nora, Violet and Jasper had set up chairs and a little table on the verandah of the Keeper's cottage, with a bottle of wine and some nibbles laid out. Juniper and Leah stood between the traffic cones at either end of the clearing. Rafe, Callum and Mikayla moved into position around John. William had just enough time to observe that this was definitely something that would never happen at one of his parent's functions before John bounced the ball into the ground, hurrying backwards out of the way as Mikayla and Callum moved in. Mikayla got first tap, knocking the ball in William's direction. He tapped it gently towards Billy. "Quick! Pick it up and kick it to Mikky!"

Everyone stood back as Billy grabbed the ball up and dropped it onto his foot, pushing at it with his toe. It rolled no more than a foot in front of him, but that was enough for Mikayla, who swooped in with a "Great kick!" before grabbing it up and hand-balling it to William. He watched as she flashed by Rafe and Callum towards their end of the ground and dropped it on his foot, sending it soaring through the air. Jesus, she was fast! She caught the ball on her chest and toed it carefully, letting it dribble across the goal line without rolling off into the scrub. William grinned from ear to ear as Juniper, face a picture of solemnity, signaled the goal. The crowd on the verandah cheered enthusiastically.

Rafe retrieved the ball and John took up the role of center umpire again. William scooped Billy up and moved into position. The bounce went Callum's way, and he quickly hand-balled the ball to Rafe, who only just barely dodged the tackle Mikayla intended to lay on him before running up the clearing and again, carefully dribbling the ball over the line. Leah indicated the goal, and the ball came back to the middle yet again. Billy squirmed to get down and they all paused to allow him to go over to Leah. Once he was safely by her side, John bounced the ball. Unhampered by Billy, William took it from Mikayla and running towards the goal, bounced it once before catching it up and toeing it over the line.

Juniper picked up the ball, grinning from ear to ear as she handed it to him. "Nice one!"

"Thanks." He felt the sweat dripping down his back, the thick air catching in his lungs.

Mikayla high fived him on the way back to the center. The next bounce went awry, causing a scrabble of feet in the dusty grass. Rafe managed to get a foot on it and send it towards the lodge and they ran as a pack after it. William, acutely aware of Leah and Billy on the goal line, scooped to pick it up and swing his foot at it, but Rafe smothered the kick, and the ball went flying towards Leah, who was now holding Billy in her arms. She saw the ball coming fast in their direction and moved her hand protectively over Billy's head, scrunching her eyes shut and turning her back, bracing herself for the impact. But then Callum was there, knocking into her slightly as he moved to intercept the ball, grabbing her around the waist as she stumbled. William's shoulders sagged with relief, but he noticed with a frown how Leah shrunk away from Callum, nodding wordlessly when he apologized and asked if she was okay.

"I just didn't want the ball to hit you."

"I know. Thank you."

It was awkward for a moment before Mikayla jogged over, taking the ball from Callum, flicking her head to send him back to the center. "You good, or you wanna go off?"

"I'm good," Leah replied, adjusting Billy on her hip.

"Great." She walked off, clapping her hands, looking at the sky. "I reckon we've got about ten more minutes. We're up twelve to six. Come on you guys, show us what you've got."

Again, John bounced the ball and it floated in William's direction. He grabbed it and headed for his goal, kicking it high, but this time, Callum was quicker, taking it in the air before it could sail over the goal line. Quick as a flash, he kicked it towards the center of the ground where Rafe was waiting. If Rafe took this mark, all he had to do was slide by Mikayla, boot it over the line and the scores would be leveled. William, too winded to run back up the ground, stood next to Juniper as the ball sailed through the air. They both gasped as Rafe, braced to catch the ball, stumbled forward slightly. Mikayla had run up behind him and taking a flying leap, braced her knees high on his back, pushed herself higher still and caught the ball on her chest, turning mid-air and gracefully landing on her feet.

"Jesus, that was amazing!" William called out. She gave him a thumbs up before booting the ball towards him. He stepped back over the line and caught it, meaning it was Mikayla's goal. As he walked back towards the center, he felt big splats of rain falling. In five seconds flat, everyone was running for the verandah and cover, but the fat drops of rain felt deliciously cool against his heated, sweaty skin so he stayed where he was, turning his face up as the clouds burst open in earnest, sending a torrent of rain cascading down on him. As if on instinct, he opened his eyes. Juniper was walking towards him, her hair hanging like ropes, her bright smile filling up all the dark, restless places inside him. Moving forward to meet her, he lost all thought of their surroundings. Cupping her beautiful face in his hands, he felt her arms come around his waist. He gazed at her for the longest moment, just drinking her in as the rain soaked them through. He then laid his lips over hers, kissing her with all the wanting, all the longing, all the need he had for her. He reveled in the feeling that she gave it all back to him tenfold. She sighed as he pulled back, then laughed as they heard Mikayla shouting at them.

"Come inside, you maniacs! You're soaked through."

He didn't care a bit.

CHAPTER 7

*W*illiam took a deep breath and let it out slowly as he finally left the snarling Sydney traffic behind him. Hitting the A1, he eased back in his seat, turning some music on and tapping to the beat. He was anticipating being back in Blessed Inlet more than he cared to admit; to the point where he had skived off the last meeting in Sydney early, citing a meeting with the builder in Blessed Inlet as an excuse. It wasn't entirely a lie. He did have a meeting with John set up. But it was at the pub—the next day. They would probably chat about the progress at the lighthouse a little.

John was very capable and efficient, and the project was flowing smoothly. The fit out of the Keeper's cottage was almost complete, they just had to rework the framing for the windows and put in some skylights in the roof. The mezzanine level for the stables was the next big project, but once that hurdle was jumped, it really was smooth sailing, with the main lodge requiring minimal work now that the flooring was fixed.

He felt a tightening in his chest as he realized what that would mean. No more Blessed Inlet. His role in the business didn't involve sticking around in a location after he'd scouted it and made it fit for purpose. Cassie took over after that and she mainly managed the onsite staff via video link. He pushed all that out of his mind, preferring to focus on what he had to look forward to in Blessed Inlet. He smiled to himself as he sped down the highway, thoughts of Juniper swirling through his mind. They'd seen as much of each other as they could since she had first spent the night, but even with their best efforts, she'd only managed to sneak in one more overnight stay before Violet had left.

After that, their encounters had been brief and opportunistic. A quick text message to say Leah was covering the shop and Billy was at a friend's house had William clearing his afternoon meetings and dragging Juniper to the bedroom as soon as she arrived. One time he'd dropped into the shop to see if she wanted lunch to find her there alone. Quick as thought, she'd locked the door, thrown up a sign saying she'd be back in thirty minutes, pulled him into the workroom, pushed him into a chair, and had her way with him. He felt his body stirring at the memory and his smile widened. He turned the music down and reached for his phone.

"Hey."

"Hey yourself." Juniper smiled into the phone. God, she'd missed him.

"I managed to get away from the meeting early, so I'm heading back now."

"Great! Do you want to come over for dinner?" She moved to the back door of the shop, checking that Leah was okay with Billy. She smiled. Billy was sitting in his Tonka truck, gripping onto the sides, while Leah, bent low, pushed him along the driveway.

"Sure. I'd love to."

She paused, thinking how best to say the next bit. "Billy will be here."

"Ah, yes, I expect he will be. He's a bit young to be heading out on the town with his mates."

She laughed. "No, I mean, you know..."

"I can't drop F bombs all night long?"

She rolled her eyes.

"I heard that."

"Heard what?"

"Your eyes roll."

She laughed again. "It's just, you know..."

"We can't have any hanky panky in the house. I know. I can't trust you to keep the noise down."

"Well, if I'm noisy, you've no one to blame but yourself."

"A cross I'm willing to bear."

God, she loved flirting with him. She also loved snuggling with him. She made a snap decision. "I tell you what. You can sleep over if you bring pajamas."

She heard him clear his throat and said hastily, "I mean, you have to wear them. All night. You can't just bring them."

He chuckled. "Dammit, I almost had you. It's a deal. I'll be there around five. You've got an air fryer?"

"Ah, yes," she said hesitantly.

"Great. I'll bring dinner."

"Oh, that's not nec—"

"See you at five." He hung up before she could protest further, and she simultaneously smiled and rolled her eyes. Her phone beeped and she looked down, seeing a text from him. She clicked into it: *Stop rolling your eyes.* Chuckling, she slipped the phone into her pocket and moved back to the pottery wheel.

~

*H*e pulled the sleek, black Porsche into her drive just after five o'clock. She watched from the loungeroom window as he got out carrying an overnight bag and two shopping bags.

The late afternoon sun added a bronzed sheen to his dark hair as he walked the few steps to her front verandah and up the stairs. "William!" Billy jumped down from his seat at the table and ran to greet him. Her heart lurched as he dropped his overnight bag and swept Billy up with one arm.

"Hey, big fella!"

"I'm playing with my frogs!"

"That's great! I want you to do something for me, though. Take all the frogs out of the pond and put them in your room."

Billy frowned, ready to object.

"Trust me."

"Okay," Billy said uncertainly, wriggling to get down.

Once he'd scooped the frogs into his shirt and ran off to his room, Juniper moved forward, relishing the light in William's eyes as they rested on her face. "Hi," she said softly, standing on tiptoe to brush her lips lightly across his. He snaked an arm around her waist, pulling her against him, turning what she'd planned to be a brief welcoming kiss into a long, lingering one that left her lips tingling when he lifted his head.

"Hi."

"I've put my frogs away!"

"Excellent. Let me put these bags down and I'll show you what I got for you." As he moved to the kitchen, he picked up the pond he'd carved for Billy and took it with him. Quickly stowing one shopping bag in the fridge, he put the other on the bench next to the pond. Intrigued, Juniper came over, lifting Billy onto one of the stools under the bench and sitting at the other one. "Now, this is a very important job. Can I trust you with it?"

Billy nodded solemnly as William removed a bag of chocolate freddo frogs from the shopping bag. "You need to open these and put them in the pond. WITHOUT eating them. Or licking them."

"Okay." Taking his job very seriously, Billy started unwrapping the first frog. Seeing that opening all twelve would be a big job for him, Juniper helped, keeping an eye on William as she did so. He was taking packs of ready-made blue jelly from the bag, placing them on the counter, and she realized straight away what he had planned. She grinned at him. It was super cute, and Billy would love it.

"Okay, good job. Now we have to get some glad wrap." He looked at Juniper enquiringly.

"Third drawer."

Retrieving the glad wrap, he carefully laid it inside the pond. "Now, open up these jellies and pour them in."

Once that was done, Billy watched as William added the first chocolate frog to the pond and his eyes went round with wonder and delight. "Chocolate frogs in my pond!" He breathed.

"That's it. Now you do the rest while I get dinner on."

Juniper got the air fryer from the cupboard and placed it on the bench, curious to see what William had planned and not setting her hopes very high. He took a bag of dinosaur shaped chicken nuggets out of the bag, reading the cooking instructions carefully.

"Seriously?" she said under her breath.

"I never joke about nuggets."

"You have the eating habits of a toddler."

"Are we having nuggets? I LOVE nuggets."

Juniper gestured to Billy as if to say, See?

William just grinned at her as he put the nuggets in the fryer and turned it on. "Not just nuggets, mate. Dino nugget wraps."

Juniper burst out laughing. He was just too much.

"Hey, they're the fancy ones. Tempura batter and everything."

"Ooh, tempura batter? Why didn't you say so!"

Laughing, William picked up the pond and put it in the fridge before organizing the fillings for the wraps. This was just lovely, thought Juniper. The way William and Billy interacted, the light banter, the affection. It was all just so...She sighed. Always, at the back of her mind was the wondering. Wondering how much longer William would be staying in Blessed Inlet. Wondering what would happen when it was time for him to go. Just wondering.

They ate the nugget wraps and although she teased him, Juniper had to admit they weren't too bad. Of course, they were a big hit with Billy so that helped. After that, it was all Juniper could do to stop Billy from eating all the chocolate frogs in the pond at once. He only gave up trying when William said that if he ate them all now, they couldn't' have any in the morning.

"Are you coming back tomorrow?" Billy asked excitedly.

William looked at Juniper. It was best for her to handle this situation. "Ah, well, baby, William's actually having a sleepover."

Billy clapped his hands in excitement. "With me?"

Juniper cleared her throat. "No, he wouldn't fit in your bed. He'll sleep with me."

"Oh, like Nana does when she comes without the car house?"

"Yes," Juniper replied, relieved. "Exactly like that."

Satisfied with that, and with a promise that he would be able to have breakfast with William if he got ready for bed with no fuss, Billy was in his pajamas, teeth brushed and in bed in no time.

"Well, that was easy," Juniper said, coming to sit with William on the couch. She snuggled in as he put his arm around her. More loveliness.

"Juniper."

Something about his tone sent a shiver of tension through her. "Yes?"

"What do you think you would do if your parents contacted you, asking to meet Billy?"

She looked at him in surprise, pulling away. "Oh, um. I don't know. Probably let them, I guess."

"Really?"

She thought about it for a very long moment, feeling a wash of hard, painful memories course through her. "I'm not sure, now that I think about it. They were just so awful when I told them I was pregnant. They didn't know I'd deliberately chosen to have a baby." She stopped, rubbing at her chest as her heart squeezed painfully. "I mean, it's one thing to not accept me, to always be uncomfortable about how different I am to them. Their world was just so foreign to me that I never felt like I was standing on solid ground. I understood that, had learned to accept it." She smiled when he took her hand in his. "But I was so ecstatic to be pregnant and I felt so lucky, so blessed. It just felt so right." Her smile turned sad. "Maybe I was a bit naïve. I thought such a blessing could maybe bring us together. That they might like the idea of being grandparents." She looked at him, taking comfort in the sympathy she could see in his eyes. "My father told me to have an abortion."

The sympathy turned to anger in flash. "What the fuck?"

"I know. That was it for me. The final dealbreaker. It wasn't like, oh, you're stuck in an awkward situation, we'll support any decision you make. It was, how would this look to their friends? How would it affect their business? Their useless, hippy, artist daughter is now a single Mum. Typical. Then my sister said I'd done it on purpose, just to upset everyone and my Mum agreed." She lifted his hand to her lips, pressing a kiss to his palm, trying to sooth him. "I rang Nana straight away, distraught. She was on the next plane to Melbourne, God love her. She tore strips off my parents, threatened to stab my sister with a fork at one point and told them all they were dead to her." She smiled, feeling lighter and easier at the memory. "But she looked after me, as well. That's when we hatched the plan for me to have the baby in Byron Bay. She flew home to get everything ready for me and the rest is history."

"Juniper, that's just so awful."

"It is, isn't it? What a pack of arseholes."

"So, after all that, if they did want to see Billy, you'd let them?"

"Maybe not. You never know the answers to those sorts of questions until you're actually presented with them. Anyway, enough of that. It's too grim."

She moved to lay her head on his shoulder, but he stopped her, tilting her head up with a finger under her chin. He leaned in to kiss her and she put her hand on his chest. "Hey."

"Hey, what? No hanky panky. Just necking."

"I know where necking leads."

"You'll just have to control yourself." He brushed his lips lightly across hers, pulling her harder against him with the arm around her shoulders. She gave in. It was exactly what she wanted, so why resist? She would just have to stop before it got out of hand, and she was ravishing him on the lounge room floor. She pushed that thought away immediately, before it gave her any serious ideas. She let herself sink into the kiss, that soft, wet tangling of tongues that she adored. She sighed, shifting closer to him, sliding her arm around his neck. Even more loveliness.

A few hours later, after they'd pretended to watch a movie but had pretty much necked all the way through it, they slid into Juniper's bed, both wearing pajamas. She sighed with contentment as he pulled her against him, spooning her, and happily drifted off to sleep.

Juniper awoke hours later to the sound of Billy climbing out of bed, his feet pattering up the hallway to her bedroom. She debated with herself whether she had the energy to get up and take him back to his bed or if she should just let him climb in, but he surprised her by going around to William's side of the bed. She lay perfectly still as she heard him whisper, "William."

He came instantly awake. "What is it, mate?" He whispered softly.

"My blanket fell off."

"Oh, you want me to take you back to bed and put it on?"

"No, it's too late."

"What do you mean?"

"My tummy's already cold. It won't get warm now."

"Oh, that's no good." Juniper could hear the smile in his whispered words. "What should we do?"

"I think I should come in there with you."

"I thought you might think that. Come on then." The mattress shifted as he made room for Billy.

Then there was quiet for a little while before Billy whispered, "Your face is scratchy." Juniper could just picture him, curled against William with his little hand lying across his cheek.

"Well, your butt's scratchy."

Billy giggled, desperately trying to keep quiet. "Tis not!"

"I'm sure it is."

"Your ear feels funny."

"That's enough now. Stop being cute and go to sleep."

A long silence, then Billy whispered, "I am cute, aren't I?"

Juniper felt the mattress shake as William laughed soundlessly. "Yes, very, but not so much at four o'clock in the morning, you little brat."

Billy giggled, then said "William?"

"Billy." The note of warning was unmistakable, even at a whisper.

"I love you."

William barely missed a beat before replying, "I love you too."

"G'night."

"Good night."

Juniper lay there for a long time, staring into the darkness, her heart full almost to bursting.

Juniper drifted through the next day on a cloud. They'd all slept in a little, cozy and quiet in her bed. Breakfast had been vastly entertaining, Billy sitting in William's lap while he ate vegemite on toast and regaled William with a story of a frog family that went into battle against evil toads. She'd brought William a coffee, relishing the soft touch of his hand on hers as she moved away. Then she'd sat down across from him to enjoy watching her son with him. He'd looked over at her as she smiled at him and went completely still, just gazing at her. She had tilted her head and looked at him questioningly, but at that moment, Billy had put his hands on William's face and brought his attention back to the story. William had left not long after that and she'd gone to open the shop. She found she couldn't concentrate, however, just drifting from task to task without completing anything properly. She'd forgotten to eat lunch, only reminded by Billy coming in from the yard to say he was starving. Then she'd got a call from Nora, asking if they could have Billy for the night and it couldn't be more perfect. So here she was, dropping him off, looking at Nora blankly when she asked if she was okay.

"Sure, of course."

"Oh, right, because you seem in a daze."

"I'm fine," she replied with a smile, giving Billy a kiss and drifting out the door to go home for a shower and a change of clothes. She made her way up to the lighthouse, seeing William's car parked out front but the whole place in total darkness. She let herself in the front door, going straight across the loungeroom to the sliding doors. She could see him silhouetted against the rising moon, his back to the house. The gentle light of the moon spilled over him, gilding him in soft, silvery light and her heart squeezed. He turned as she crossed to him, opening his arms. She stepped into them, pressing her lips against his. She sank into it, pressing herself against him, deepening the kiss, toying with his tongue. She sighed as his hands moved up to the zipper of her dress, sliding it down ever so slowly. Then the tips of his fingers were caressing her back, a featherlight touch. She moved her hands to the buttons of his shirt, undoing them slowly then pushing the shirt aside to run her hands over his chest. She kicked off her shoes and shrugged out of the dress, letting it fall to the ground, standing naked before him, feeling a rush of warmth course through her as he looked at her, his eyes shadowy in the light of the moon. She slid her hands down to the button of his pants, undoing it and pushing his pants down. He stepped out of them as she slid the shirt down his arms and off. They were both naked, flesh pressed against flesh, the moon their only witness. With one arm around his neck, she slid her palm down his chest, smiling as she felt him quivering as she took his cock in her hand, stroking it as she watched him, the pleasure in his eyes inflaming her. He wrapped his fingers around her wrist and pulled her hand away and she knew, like her, he wanted the moment to last. He lowered himself to sit on the cool grass and she went with him, straddling him as he wrapped his arms around her, pressing soft, wet kisses along her jawline, neck, collar bone. She pushed her fingers into his hair and pulled his head back, taking his lips with hers in a long, drugging kiss.

She shifted until she could feel the head of his cock pressing against her. She leaned back a little to watch him as she lowered herself onto him, sighing at the pure, hot pleasure of him filling her. With her fingers linked behind his neck she leaned back further, delighted when he moved his hands to cover her breasts, kneading and squeezing, toying with her nipples. She moaned softly, wanting his tongue in her mouth again, taking it, taking him further inside her as she increased the rhythm of her hips. As the pressure increased, as the heat built, she draped her arm across his shoulders and with her other hand, cupped his cheek.

"William," she said softly as she moved faster on him. "William, oh god." She dropped her forehead on his as she let her body go, grinding her hips on him faster and faster until she climaxed, feeling him go rigid against her, his arms tightening around her, holding her still as he exploded inside her. Breathless, her heart thumping hard against her rib cage, she rested her head on his shoulder.

As her heart rate slowed and she got her breath back, she lifted her head to look at him in the moonlight, reaching up to brush his hair back from his forehead tenderly.

"I love you," they said at the same time, and they smiled. She kissed him. "Say it again," she said softly.

"I love you."

"I love you, too." She wrapped her arms around him and pressed her face against his neck, just breathing him in.

He ran his hands gently up and down her back. "Do you want to know when I knew?"

"This morning at breakfast."

He laughed softly. "How did you know?"

"Because you were looking at me funny, but something in your eyes was mirroring how I was feeling. I realized last night, when I heard you with Billy."

"Oh, you were awake, were you?"

"Yes, it was the cutest thing I've ever heard." She lifted her head and looked at him. "I mean, if a woman can't love a man who tells her kid he has a scratchy butt, the world is lost, no?"

He laughed then, pushing his fingers into her hair and pulling her to him for a long, lingering kiss. "Christ, I adore you."

"Ditto."

"Can you stay the night?"

"Yes, but I forgot to bring an overnight bag." She shifted off him and rose to her feet, reaching for her dress.

"I notice you forgot to wear underwear, too."

She grinned. "Oh no, that was deliberate." She slipped the dress over her head as he pulled his pants on before they headed inside.

"Have you eaten?"

"No, but you'd better not offer me spaghetti toasties." She said, following him to the kitchen.

"Wouldn't dream of it," he replied, looking through the pantry cupboard and pulling out a foil pouch of fresh vegetable soup. "This, with toast?"

"Perfect." She boosted up to sit on the bench while he made dinner. With the soup warming on the stove and the bread in the toaster, he turned and leaned back against the counter, crossing his arms over his chest, looking across the kitchen at her.

God, she was a miracle, sitting in his kitchen, swinging her legs, her fingers linked loosely, resting in her lap. Smiling her beautiful smile. "I love you." The words felt perfect on his lips, perfect in his heart. Her eyes glowed, warming him.

"I love you."

"I want you to meet my family."

A look flickered across her face, quickly smothered and hard to read.

"I know they'll love you, but I don't want to pressure you," he reassured her.

She took a deep breath. "Okay." Her fingers clenched and he could see the knuckles whiten.

He moved across the kitchen, cupping her face in his hands and brushing his lips across hers. "There's nothing to be anxious about, I promise you."

Her green eyes cloudy, she took another deep breath. "Of course. It's okay. It'll be lovely."

He pressed a kiss to her forehead and moved away to take care of dinner.

～

*J*uniper did her best to push down the little ball of anxiety in the pit of her stomach. She glanced at William, sitting comfortably as he tooled the Porsche through the Sydney streets. She felt the buildings closing in on her, the traffic congestion smothering her, the noise and smell invading her senses. She really did hate being in the city. Give her the pristine beach and fresh air of Blessed Inlet any day of the week. It wasn't just the urban landscape troubling her, though. They were due to meet William's family for lunch at twelve thirty, which she was quite looking forward to. It was the evening engagement that was feeding the ball of anxiety in her gut. Their visit was coinciding with a function William's mother had organized to schmooze some corporate clients. It was exactly the kind of event her parents excelled at. They loved plastering those fake, frozen smiles on their faces and wining and dining. She may not have minded it, except that she was terrible at it, incapable of doing the business small talk, the fake interest, knowing what topics to avoid, which topics to specifically bring up with which person. She looked out the window as they drove down Henry Lawson Avenue, forcing her hands to unclench. She could do it. This wasn't like when she was young and single, going to these events on her own time and time again. She was older, wiser, more confident. William would be there. Plus, it was only one night.

"All good?"

"Sure." She'd hardly spoken since they'd hit the outskirts of Sydney and she knew he'd noticed. God, why couldn't she just get over it? She leaned forward to look through the windscreen at the boutique hotel nestled on the water's edge at Lavender Bay. It was a tall, elegant column, all steel and thickened glass. Modern and chic. William steered the Porsche around the circular drive to the front of the hotel and parking, got out, handing the keys to the uniformed valet who had stepped forward with alacrity.

"Mr. Locke."

"Good morning, Geoffrey. Are my parents in?"

"Not yet, sir."

"Have me notified when they arrive."

"Yes, sir," he replied as he moved around to Juniper's side of the car, opening the door for her. William put his hand on the small of her back as they walked through into the hotel lobby. It was expensive, was her first thought. Polished terrazzo flooring, long low creamy leather couches. Mixed in amongst the starkly modern furniture were antiques, juxtaposing the old with the new perfectly. William moved to the reception desk to give instructions for lunch before leading her to the bank of elevators. They whizzed up to the penthouse and she gasped as the elevator doors slid open directly into the suite. The floor-to-ceiling windows framed a view of the Sydney Harbor Bridge, the Opera House, the iconic bay with its green and yellow ferries chugging back and forth, and Luna Park.

"Wow."

William smiled at her. "It's pretty great, hey. I never get sick of it."

"It's amazing. It's all amazing." She looked around at the suite, decorated in a soft palette of creams and beiges, elegant artwork adorning the walls, plump comfortable sofas facing a big screen television, antique coffee tables and side buffets filling out the rest of the space. "So this is where you live? All the time?" Somehow, she'd never realized he lived in a hotel permanently.

"Yes."

There was no kitchen, just an antique buffet with a kettle, mini fridge and coffee machine. "Where do you keep the jaffle maker?"

He walked over to the buffet, opening one of the doors, waving his hand with a flourish. Inside was a jaffle maker, a bread bin and several cans of spaghetti. She burst out laughing and he grinned at her.

The elevator dinged, the doors opening to show a uniformed bellhop with their bags. Juniper moved to the windows as William dealt with the bellhop. Once he'd left, William came up behind her, wrapping his arms around her waist and pulling her against him. She sighed, leaning back and covering his hands with her own.

"I wonder what Billy is up to right now."

"Playing in John's workshop and wheedling cookies out of Nora," William laughed.

Juniper sighed. "Probably."

William kissed the top of her head. "We could have brought him with us."

She shook her head. "No, this first time it's better if he's safe." She regretted her choice of words as soon as she felt him stiffen behind her. He turned her to face him, crooking his finger under her chin when she tried to avoid his gaze. He searched her face for a long moment, concern and confusion clear in his eyes. Safe was a strange choice of words, she knew, seeing as how Billy would hardly be in danger with William's family in Sydney. The point, however, that she was barely acknowledging even to herself, was that she didn't feel safe. She felt a bit overwhelmed, anxious, cornered. She felt worried about the evening party, worried about how they were going to resolve their future together. Neither of them had really talked about it, mainly because she was avoiding it, what with their love still being a relatively new acknowledgement between them. But she knew that she wanted to marry him, spend her life with him, have his babies. She didn't think she could do any of that in Sydney though, and there was the rub. She searched her mind for the right words to explain these feelings, but to her surprise, he leaned forward and brushed a tender kiss across her lips.

"I love you."

It was the best reassurance he could give her. "I love you, too." She smiled, "I'd better get changed."

"You look fine as you are," he protested.

She looked down at her dress, the soft floaty skirt in a rich berry red, the ties across the bodice, the puff sleeves. It was the sort of dress she wore all the time at home, but it wasn't exactly Sydney chic. "That's sweet," she said, "but no. I won't be long."

She emerged from the bedroom twenty minutes later in grey slacks, a soft pink cashmere sweater with a boat neck, and low-heeled sandals. She'd tied her hair in a low ponytail and included silver hoop earrings. Minimal makeup completed the look. William turned from the window as she stepped out of the bedroom, looking her up and down. "Nice," he said.

A certain note in his voice caught her. Pulling at the waistband of the sweater nervously, she said, "No?"

"Huh? You look great."

"Oh, it's just, you didn't sound…"

He looked at her for a long moment, considering. "You look perfect, just…different."

She was saved from answering by the intercom beeping, advising William that his family had arrived.

CHAPTER 8

*W*illiam gave Juniper's hand a reassuring squeeze as they rode the elevator to the rooftop terrace. Although she was pretty much an open book to him, generally sharing her thoughts and feelings unreservedly, he was struggling a little to read her at the moment and it bothered him. He let go of the concern for now as they stepped out onto the terrace. A table was set with a snowy white cloth and an elegant setting nestled beneath a shade sail, offering stunning views of the bridge and opera house. His mother, sister and sister's partner rose to their feet and William's heart swelled at the chance to finally introduce his family to Juniper. His mother was the first to step forward, a welcoming smile on her face. She looked impeccable as always, her grey hair pulled back neatly in a French knot, her slim form clad in a sleeveless black dress, fancy high heels on her feet.

"Juniper! It's an absolute pleasure to meet you."

"Thank you," Juniper said, shaking her hand in return. Then Cassie and her partner James came forward and shook hands.

William moved over to his father, who reached out with his left hand, gripping William hard around the wrist. "Help me up, son."

"Dad, that's not necessary."

"Important moment. Help me up."

His father had that steely note in his voice, even though his speech was slurred, that brooked no argument, so William obeyed, hefting his father to his feet with an arm hard around his waist. He waited until Robert had steadied himself with his walking frame before stepping back slightly to allow Juniper to step forward. Because Robert was mostly paralyzed on his right side and was therefore leaning on his frame with his left hand, it made it impossible for him to shake Juniper's hand without losing his balance. It was one of the adjustments he'd had to make since the stroke, a new way of navigating these sorts of social situations. William knew that Robert hated it, especially that awkward moment when people first met him and weren't sure how to greet him, since the habitual handshake was not an option. But Juniper solved that issue easily by stepping right up to him, placing her hands on his shoulders, and pressing a warm kiss to his cheek.

"I'm very pleased to meet you," she said with a smile.

"Likewise." Robert was so obviously delighted with her that it warmed William's heart. He helped his father back into his chair at the head of the table, before taking the seat at his right hand, his mother sitting opposite William. This tag teaming with his mother to look after his father was a familiar routine when William was home. The transition from fully fit, functioning businessman to reliant invalid had struck Robert hard and William tried as hard as he could to inure his father to the worst of it whenever he could. He knew his mother did the same, as evidenced by her current focus on making him comfortable. Once William could see that Robert was settled, he leaned back against the bench seat, laying his arm along the back of the seat, resting his fingertips lightly on Juniper's shoulder.

Cassie, sitting at the foot of the table, picked up her wine glass and turning in her chair, said, "So, Juniper, full disclosure here. You're the first girlfriend of William's we've met in, what is it, Mum? A decade?"

Gwen nodded. "It must be about that long."

"Lord, wasn't she a sour faced piece of work. I can't even remember her name. You're so much better."

"Um, thank you."

"But we have a problem; William has told us barely anything about you. How did you two meet?"

Juniper looked at William, a little stumped. It wasn't that he deliberately hadn't told them, it was just that moments after Billy had been born, he'd found out about his father's stroke. With all that dealing with that had entailed in the months afterwards, it hadn't really come up. Then when he had met her again, he had kept her to himself. He wasn't sure exactly why. Maybe at the time, it had just felt too big to share, or too uncertain.

"Well, that's quite a story, actually," he said, pouring more wine for himself and Juniper and juice for his father.

"Right, let's get the entrée served before you start, so we aren't interrupted," Gwen said. As they ate an entrée of crisp bread rolls and Vichyssoise, the conversation remained superficial, covering the weather and the upcoming football season. Once they were all finished and the bowls removed, Cassie linked her fingers through James's, propping her chin on her other hand and looking expectantly at William. He relayed the story, finishing with seeing Juniper on the beach a week or so after returning to Blessed Inlet.

Cassie sighed. "That's like fate. How beautiful."

"So, Juniper, what's his name? You're little boy?" Gwen asked with a smile.

"William," she said simply, looking at William with that glow in her eyes that warmed him to his core. "But we call him Billy."

"He's named after William, then?" Cassie confirmed.

"He is."

"This is the best story I have ever heard. I'll be having words with you later, William Locke, for not sharing it earlier."

"What's he like?" Gwen asked.

"He's a scoundrel," William said with a smile.

"Oh, my favorite kind of kid!"

Juniper laughed. "He can be a scoundrel, but he's incredibly sweet and loving. He adores William."

"The feeling's mutual."

"He can't get enough of the frogs he made him for his birthday."

"Huh?"

William's heart sank at Cassie's look of bewilderment. Juniper looked at her, confused.

"Frogs William made?" Cassie clarified.

"Yes. He carved them out of wood, with the pond and every-thing. It's pretty much the only toy Billy plays with most days."

"William carved frogs from wood?"

Juniper was clearly struggling with Cassie's confusion. "Ah, yes."

"I didn't know you could do that."

Reaching for his wine and taking a sip, William shrugged.

"Well, he can. He's very good at it, actually." Juniper laid her hand over his where it rested on her shoulder, offering a word-less apology for causing him discomfort. She had no way of knowing that his family weren't aware of his hobby. He hadn't picked up a chisel or carving knife in over twenty years, after all.

"Hm, interesting. You're full of secrets, aren't you, brother of mine?" Cassie said, flicking him a look.

William squirmed. He hadn't been deliberately secretive; it had just never come up and the Lockes didn't really indulge in hobbies outside of golf. Until he'd been to Blessed Inlet, it hadn't even occurred to him that he might be talented in anything other than the family trade.

"Well, enough of that," Gwen cut in, rescuing William. "William also tells us that you make pottery, Juniper."

"I do, yes."

"And you have a shop?"

"Yes."

"That must be lovely."

"It is. There's a little house attached to the back of the shop, so it makes it easy for me to have Billy with me while I'm working."

"Do you think you'll have a shop in Sydney?"

The tension that seized Juniper at his mother's words was palpable. "Ah, I'm not really sure," she prevaricated.

"Oh, it would be a shame to give it up just because you've moved," Gwen opined.

"We haven't really talked about any of that, Mum."

"Oh, I see." There was a long, awkward pause. "Well, I'm sure you'll figure it out." She smiled reassuringly at Juniper. "How about we move on to the main course."

"Great idea," said Cassie. "Honey, why don't you tell William the latest with the buyout at your work." James, taking the hint with alacrity, launched into the latest tidbit in the ongoing saga at the company he'd worked at for over a decade.

For the main course, they enjoyed salmon wellington with a green bean salad and buttery baby potatoes. Everyone agreed on a break before dessert. William followed Juniper as she walked over to the railing overlooking the harbor. He slipped an arm around her waist, and she leaned into him, smelling of flowers and sunshine and something so indescribably her. "I'm sorry about that, before."

Juniper sighed. She didn't blame his mother for the assumption that she would move to Sydney. It was clear as crystal that William's commitment to his family and their business meant him living in Sydney. "That's okay, it's not their fault. It's a reasonable assumption to make."

He was quiet for a moment, and she glanced up at him. There was that shuttered expression so she couldn't be sure what he was thinking. Then he looked down at her and smiled. "We'll figure it out."

She took the reassurance, even though she couldn't really see how exactly they would do that. She kissed him. "I love you." She would never get sick of seeing that light in his eyes when he heard those words from her.

"I love you, too." The light turned to a wicked gleam on a heart-beat. "Maybe we could go for a swim after this? I can lock up the pool house so no one can come in. We can skinny dip."

She laughed. "Sounds good to me."

"Alright, you cute kids, look over here for me, would you?"

They both turned to see Cassie pointing her phone camera at them. "Just a quick snap for Aunty Laura, if you don't mind."

"Sure."

She took the picture, then told William that their dad wanted a word with him. Stepping up next to Juniper at the railing as William moved away, she pushed her fingers through her long, brown hair. "I can't tell you what it means to us to have you here."

"Oh, thank you. It's a pleasure for me to be here and finally meeting all of you. William's told me so much about you."

"It interests me that he hadn't told us too much about you and Billy before today." She surveyed her brother for a long moment. "Still waters run deep, as the saying goes." She turned to study Juniper, her astute brown eyes missing nothing. Juniper returned her gaze calmly, quite enjoying this frank, open woman who obviously loved her brother very much. Cassie grinned then, saying, "Mum's itching to get over here and talk to you so I'm going to stand here a little longer, pretending to be deep in conversation, to torment her a little."

Cassie proceeded to chat amiably for the next few minutes, much to Juniper's amusement. "Right, she's ready to slay me, I'd better be off." With that she moved over to sit in James's lap, finally giving her mother the chance she was desperate for. Gwen jumped on it quickly, bringing two glasses of chilled white wine with her. Handing Juniper one of the glasses with a smile, she didn't speak at first, instead turning and watching William and his father. Juniper followed her gaze, seeing them sitting side by side, deep in conversation. The respect and affection between them was so obvious it caused Juniper's heart to flutter nervously. There was simply no way William could not live in Sydney. His father needed him too much. She turned away, looking out over the harbor, letting the idea play out. The idea of moving to Sydney. Of packing up her shop, selling it and the house, of dragging Billy away from everything he knew and loved. The idea sat like a ball of lead in her belly, but if she was honest with herself, she couldn't really see another way. If they wanted to be together, one of them would have to make the move and it was becoming increasingly obvious that of the two of them, it was more of a possibility for her than it was for him, logistics wise.

"He seems different."

"Does he?" Juniper asked, recognizing that Gwen was referring to William.

"Yes. In the best possible way." She turned away from watching her husband and son, looking Juniper full in the face, her blue eyes shining. "It's because of you, of course. I can't tell you how happy it makes me." She reached out and rubbed her hand affectionately up and down Juniper's arm. "I'll be honest with you. I've been a bit worried about him over the last few years." She paused, taking a sip of wine and leaning against the railing. "What would it have been, maybe three or four years ago? Yes, that feels right. I just noticed something was off with him. I'd ask about it and he'd just smile and say he didn't know what I was talking about. Then of course, Robert's stroke changed everything, taking all of my focus. Taking all of ours', really. And William was just amazing throughout. He's our rock and we're grateful every day for him. I know that sounds dramatic, but I don't think it can be overstated. After the initial shock of Robert's stroke wore off and we settled into the new normal, understanding that how he is now is pretty much as good as he was likely to get, it was awful. The one thing that grounded Robert and kept him holding on was the family business. He and I have spent decades building it up and being able to bring the kids into it when they were old enough, to be able to give them that security in life, meant so much to us. The idea that with his stroke we would have to let it go, was crushing. But William said no, we'll work around it. We'll change things up. He works so hard to make sure Robert is still as involved as he can be in the day to day running of it, knowing that it gives Robert that purpose, that focus that he needs." She paused and the silence spun out a little before she said, very quietly, "I'm not sure he can do that from Blessed Inlet."

"I understand."

Gwen sighed with relief. "I just so hope you can sort it out, darling, because I don't think I've ever seen William so happy. Or content is probably a better word. At peace. I look at you both and I just want you to be happy, to be able to build a life together." Her eyes welled with tears. "Oh god, now I'm being melodramatic. I'm sorry." She reached over to the nearby table and, grabbing a napkin, dabbed at her eyes.

"Don't be sorry. It's lovely that you feel that way." Juniper spent a fleeting moment comparing William's mother's wishes for him, versus her own for her. They were light years apart and the realization made her feel a surge of affection for Gwen. On impulse, she reached out and put her arms around Gwen, who hugged her right back.

"You are just the most beautiful girl." She pulled back, kissing Juniper on the cheek. "Now I'm going to leave you alone before I freak you out anymore." She moved over to Robert, letting him know that it was time to go and rest before the evening's function. After Gwen and Robert left, Juniper and William sat with Cassie and James for a while, eating tri-chocolate terrine for dessert, chatting and enjoying the afternoon sunshine. Then William was pulling Juniper away, down to the indoor pool. He locked the door and of course they made love, just as he'd planned.

~

*J*uniper sat at the little dresser in the bedroom wearing her bathrobe, with a towel wrapped around her head, carefully applying her makeup. A bit heavier than what she'd worn for lunch, so it needed a bit more work. She hardly ever wore makeup these days, the consequence being that she felt out of practice, and it was making her nervy. William was pulling on his tuxedo jacket, and she paused to watch him. He looked very dashing as he slid the black bowtie around his neck. He caught her watching him in the mirror and smiled. "Gotta love a monkey suit," he said. He did look very dashing, yet somehow, weirdly, unfamiliar. She smiled wordlessly and turned back to the mirror. He came over and pressing a kiss to her cheek, said he'd be waiting in the lounge area for her.

Some forty minutes later, she felt more than a little flustered. Her hair had been impossible, no matter how much product she put in it. She just couldn't seem to get the curls under control, so she had settled for a tight, low bun, containing them as best she could. Added to that, she'd put a ladder in her stockings as she pulled them on so there was no choice but to go without, which felt weird. Taking a deep breath and forcing her fingers to unclench, she opened the bedroom door and stepped into the loungeroom. William looked up from his seat on the couch and gave a low whistle.

"You look amazing."

She smiled, turning a circle in front of him as he rose to his feet. "Weekend wardrobe courtesy of Leah. I don't have anything in my closet even remotely appropriate for this sort of thing." She caught a glimpse of her reflection in the tall windows. She wore an off the shoulder column dress in a shimmering silver fabric and silver strappy heels. For a fleeting moment she had the feeling that she was looking at a complete stranger, so she turned away. "Should we go?"

"Yep, if you're ready."

She was as ready as she would ever be. As they stepped into the elevator, she shivered. Because the event was being held in the function hall in the hotel, she hadn't thought to include a wrap or cardigan with her outfit. She held tight to William's hand as they walked across the lobby and through the doors into the function room. It was exactly as she expected. A stage at the far end was set up with a band playing, the bluesy notes floating lightly over the crowd. The women in glittering jewelry and beautiful gowns, the men impeccable in tuxedos and shiny shoes. The soft murmur of conversation, the delicate clinking of glasses. A waiter clad in a white jacket glided up to them with a tray of glasses filled with champagne and Juniper took one gratefully. The time to schmooze was upon her and she needed all the fortification she could get. Her heart was thudding painfully against her rib cage, and she just managed to resist the urge to press her hand there to try and calm it.

Cassie spotted them and came over. "Juniper! You look smashing!"

"So do you."

Cassie looked lovely, dressed in a lemon-colored dress with a ballerina skirt and sweetheart neckline, her chestnut hair piled high on her head in an artfully messy knot. On most women it would look too girly, but something about Cassie's businesslike flare forestalled that. "Come with me, there's someone I really want you to meet."

"Cassie—"

"What? I'll look after her." Cassie rolled her eyes at William before grabbing Juniper by the arm. It was impossible to resist her, so Juniper shot a strained smile at William before being dragged away. "I'm so excited. I was checking out your website this afternoon, after lunch, and I was thinking that hand painted stuff you sell is really something. Mum collects art so I know a bit about it. There's this friend of hers, Martha, who is always looking for new talent. That's her, over there in that hideous red dress. So avant-garde, you know." Her laughter tinkled on the air as she pulled Juniper along. "Martha! Darling! So good to see you." Air kiss, air kiss. "There's someone I want you to meet.

This is Juniper!" She presented Juniper with a flourish and Martha gave her a smile that bordered on a sneer.

"Delighted," she said. She was a tall woman, clad in a red wrap dress, her black hair swept up in a beehive 'do with a streak of red across the front.

"Juniper is an artist. Ssh, you are!" Cassie continued, smothering Juniper's feeble protest.

"Oh, is that so? Which art school did you attend?"

"I didn't, I ah…" Martha had raised her eyebrows with a look of such disdain on her face that the words Juniper had been about to utter died on her lips.

"Martha! There's no need to look like that. Once you see what I'm talking about you'll be all over Juniper like a rash." She turned to Juniper. "Do you have a business card?" Juniper shook her head, not misreading Cassie's flash of disappointment. "Right, well, I'll be in touch, Martha. Trust me, you won't be disappointed." Martha nodded, and with a thin smile, turned away to greet someone else. "Oh, sorry about that. I forgot she could be such a cow. But she's got the best eye in the business and if she takes you on, you're set."

"But I don't really want to be taken on," Juniper protested.

"Nonsense! Imagine the volume you could sell if someone like Martha Wainwright was sponsoring you."

Juniper could just imagine it and it made her feel more stressed and anxious than she already was. She loved her little shop, loved her work, loved working with Leah. It gave her the perfect work/life balance. But she could see that there was no way of explaining that to Cassie, ever the businesswoman, looking for an opportunity behind every nook and cranny and if she couldn't find it, she would make it happen. Cassie looked around the room, her eyes narrowing, obviously looking for who else she could introduce Juniper to. Gwen swept up at that moment, rescuing Juniper from one horror only to plunge her into another. A group of women; gathered together, turned to her as one when she approached with Gwen, there was no nastiness, it wasn't rude, she could tell. Gwen had obviously told them she was there with William, and they were interested and curious. However, she felt like she was under a microscope with the way they were all inspecting her. They asked lots of friendly questions about where she lived, for details on how she and William had met, about Billy. A waiter came by, and she placed her half empty champagne glass on the tray. Her fingers were tingling so she didn't think she should have any more.

It was with immense relief that she saw William approach. "That's enough, Mum," he said with a laugh. "It's my turn to show her off now." She fought the urge to snap at him that she wasn't a piece of art, to be shown off. He slipped her arm through his and squeezed her fingers as he led her away. "Everything okay?"

"Sure."

He stopped walking and looked down at her. "Are you sure, because you look a little pale?"

"No, it's fine. I'm just not that great at these sorts of things."

"You're doing fine." He pulled her over to yet another group of people and made the introductions. She fixed that frozen smile on her face and tried not to grit her teeth as she answered all of their questions. The conversation led, as it inevitably did at these sorts of functions, to what she did for a living. She answered and then the next round of questions – how many shops did she have? Oh, just one? What was her plan for expansion? Did she have an internet presence? Who managed her social media? Did she have top insurance cover for couriering her internet sales?

"Everyone, settle down. She's boutique," William said with a laugh. She looked up at him, a little startled at the dismissive tone she thought she detected. He grinned down at her, rubbing his hand up and down her back. He had that schmoozing, networking face they all seemed to wear, that slickness she'd first detected when she'd met him again on the beach. She felt like a curtain had fallen between them, thick and heavy. He leaned in, saying quietly, "I just need to go and check on my father. You'll be alright for a minute?"

She nodded and he walked away, leaving her. God, she felt so thirsty. She took a glass of champagne one of William's friends handed her, taking a long sip, but quickly placing it on the tray of a passing waiter. Her fingers really were tingling now. The sensation was disconcerting. She was trembling all over. "Are you alright?" One of the women asked her.

"Yes, I just have to..." she moved away, letting the sentence hang in the air. She needed to find the bathroom, splash some water on her face, calm her nerves. She looked around frantically as the noise around her seemed to increase, pulsing inside her head, rushing in her ears. She spied the bathroom sign and moved frantically towards it, pushing at the door, pressing her back against it once she was through. She felt warm all over all of a sudden and moved to the sinks, ran the cold tap over her hands, ready to splash on her face. She looked up, into the mirror. The person looking back at her didn't look like her. The slicked down hair, the heavy makeup, the fancy dress. She felt a constriction in her throat, her breath coming in shallow gasps.

Her heart hammered hard against her ribs. Her blood rushed in her ears, louder than ever. So loud it was causing her head to ache. She couldn't get her breath and the woman in the mirror looked back at her, a stricken look in her eyes.

Dimly aware of the bathroom door opening, of laughing chatter, she turned away, looking in her little clutch bag for her lipstick, trying to look busy, like she wasn't falling to pieces.

"Juniper?"

She stared at Gwen standing next to her, her face a weird white blob.

"Cassie, get William! Come on darling, it's okay. Sit down here." Gwen put an arm around Juniper's waist and guided her to a big couch in the center of the bathroom. She couldn't get her breath. She could hear her heartbeat in her ears, muffling Gwen's words. Maybe she was dying? Was she dying? Billy. She felt the hot sting of tears in her eyes. Then William was there, kneeling in front of her, trying to take her freezing cold hands in his. She pushed him away. She was dying. She could see stars. Billy.

"Juniper!" William shook her roughly, pulling her attention to him. She looked at him. He seemed miles away, down a long tunnel. "Honey, breathe." It was the endearment that pulled her back, just enough for her to be able to listen to him. "You're alright. Just breathe. That's it. You're doing great." His words were soft and soothing, offering encouragement.

She'd heard his voice before, just like that. When she was having Billy. She remembered. "William," she whispered brokenly.

"I'm here, honey. I've got you. Just breathe a little more. Yeah, like that."

She took one long breath after another, never taking her eyes off him. The rushing in her ears was subsiding. Her heart wasn't hitting her ribcage quite so hard. He took her hands and chafed at them with his own. "Get her some water, Cass."

"Maybe we should call an ambulance."

William shifted to sit on the sofa next to her as Cassie brought a glass of water. Oh, that's right. She was thirsty. She took a long drink. "God, she's like ice." He took his jacket off and laid it over her shoulders, pulling her against him. She pressed her face into his neck as his arms came around her. "She's shaking like a leaf."

"We have to get her out of here," Gwen said, taking the glass from Juniper's hand before she dropped it.

God, yes. There was absolutely no way she could face all those people again.

"I can't carry her, it would draw too much attention, but I'm not sure she can walk."

"I can walk," she said, her voice reed thin even to her own ears.

"I've got an idea. I'll start the speeches early. Mum, you run interference between here and the main doors. William, you help Juniper."

"Good plan. Let's go."

"I'm so sorry."

Gwen bent down and kissed Juniper on the forehead. "Don't you dare start that. You just let William look after you."

William helped Juniper to her feet, feeling a little shaky himself. God, she'd scared the shit out of him. He'd never seen her like that. Her face pale as death, her eyes enormous and dark and that choking sound she had been making when he got to the bathroom. He'd almost rather help her give birth again than watch her go through that. "Come on, honey." With his arm around her waist, William half carried Juniper out the door that Gwen was holding open for them. Cassie had successfully pulled everyone's attention away from the main doors by taking to the stage.

They were up in the suite in no time. He sat her down on the couch and went to the drinks trolley and poured her a straight brandy. She shook her head when he held it out to her. "Take it. You'll feel better." She looked up at him, her eyes huge and haunted, her face still deathly pale. "Take it, honey, please." She took it and knocked it back in one shot, wincing as she handed the glass back to him. It seemed to bring a little color back to her cheeks and her hands were shaking less. "Come on. I know what you need."

He led her to the bathroom, running the shower as hot as he thought she could stand. Then he removed the pins from her hair, running his fingers through it to loosen it, kneeling to remove her shoes, helping her out of the dress. Then he quickly stripped off and stepped into the shower, pulling her with him. He wrapped his arms around her, and she sighed as the hot water washed over her. He stroked her hair gently and kissed the top of her head. She made a sound, a half-strangled sob and he tightened his hold. "Let it out, honey."

She did, wrapping her arms around his neck, burying her face in his neck and bawling her eyes out. There was nothing he could do but hold her while she rode it out, so that's what he did.

She took a deep, shuddering breath as the sobs subsided. "I'm so sorry."

"Don't say that."

"I feel like such an idiot."

"Don't say that either."

"I didn't look like me. Isn't that stupid? I got so upset because I looked in the mirror and I didn't look like me."

He understood what she meant because although she had looked absolutely lovely and perfect for the occasion, she really didn't look anything like he was used to seeing her, with her crazy curls that he loved so much and her flower child dresses. He leaned back a little but she kept her head down so he crooked a finger under her chin, tilting her face up to his. His heart cracked a little at the expression in her eyes. Desolate was the word that came to mind. Not knowing what else to do, he reached for the shampoo, squirting some in his palm and rubbing his hands together before pushing his fingers into her hair, washing it and giving her scalp a massage at the same time. At least he could wash the gunk out for her.

When he was finished, he turned the taps off and reached for a towel, wrapping it around her before getting one for himself. He got another towel and squeezed as much water out of her hair as he could then he dried them both off and led her to the bed.

Once under the covers, she nestled against him. At least she wasn't bone chillingly cold anymore. They were lying face to face, he had one arm under her pillow and the other resting lightly on her hip. She wriggled closer, hooking her leg over him, sighing as she pushed her fingers into his hair, searching for his lips with her own.

"Juniper?"

"Please, William."

He couldn't resist her. He didn't want to resist her. Sliding his hand from her hip, up her back, into her hair, he kissed her. She pushed her tongue into his mouth a little desperately, but he slowed her down, kissing her with heartbreaking tenderness. He swept his hand down her body in soft, soothing strokes. She sighed into his mouth as his hand found her breast, cupping her gently. He eased her onto her back, just giving her those soft, drugging kisses for the longest time before breaking away, pressing light, wet kisses down her neck, across her breasts, down her stomach until he was nestled between her legs. He ran his tongue lightly over her clitoris, his senses filled with the taste of her, the scent of her, this woman who he loved so much. He worked on her until he felt the tension building within her, pushing her until the pleasure cascaded through her and she came with a soft sigh. Then he moved up her body until he was kissing her again, tangling his tongue with hers so she could taste herself. She wrapped her arms and legs around him, clinging to him, and he slipped inside her, all warm and wet as she was. He never stopped kissing her as he moved inside her, pushing her up again with long, deep strokes until she stiffened against him, her head falling back against his arm, her legs tightening around his waist. Only then did he let himself go.

After a little while, he rolled off her onto his back. He pulled her against his side and she rested her head on his shoulder, placing her hand over his still thudding heart. He listened as her breathing deepened and she drifted off to sleep. But he couldn't sleep. He lay there staring into the darkness, a slick ball of dread building in his gut, leaving a bitter taste in his mouth.

CHAPTER 9

"*Y*ou're different here." She said quietly without looking at him. She was staring out over the harbor, her robe pulled tight as she sat across the breakfast table from him, not touching her food.

"Am I?"

She nodded, keeping her gaze averted. He wanted to push her, but he was too afraid he knew what she meant, so he let it lie.

"Mum's already texted this morning, asking after you."

"What did you tell her?"

"That you were much better, but that you really wanted to get home to Billy, so we were going to make an early start."

"That's good."

"Maybe you could eat a little bit of breakfast, at least, before we go."

She picked up her fork, pushing the poached egg around on her plate.

"Juniper."

She glanced up at him, then quickly away. He sighed. He had no idea what he'd been going to say, anyway.

He leaned back in his chair, one hand in his pocket, the other wrapped around his coffee mug, his own plate of food virtually untouched. She managed to force down a little to eat before pushing her chair back and rising to her feet. He looked up quickly as she came around to his side of the table. The look in her eyes nearly broke his heart as she bent down and pressed a soft kiss to his lips.

"I love you."

He managed to speak around the lump in his throat. "I love you, too." He moved to put his arm around her, but she shifted away.

"I'll just get my things. I'd really like to go home now."

"Okay."

The drive back to Blessed Inlet seemed to take forever. He usually didn't mind it, just cruising in the Porsche, maybe playing a bit of music, usually thinking about Juniper. But there was no festive mood in the car, just a somber quiet, with Juniper curled up in her seat, staring out the window. When they finally pulled up in her drive, she got out of the car wordlessly, waiting at the trunk for him to open it. She took her case from him.

"Juniper." He couldn't disguise the pleading note in his voice. "Are you angry with me?" That finally got her looking at him.

"No, of course not."

Well, that was a relief, but then it made him more concerned. "Then why are you avoiding me? You won't look at me, you've barely touched me since we got up this morning."

"Because if I touch you, I'll want to hold you, and if I hold you, I won't be able to let you go."

"Jesus, Juniper, don't talk like that."

She sighed, closing the gap between them and wrapping her arms tight around his neck. He squeezed her tight against him, not wanting to let go. She pulled back first, looking up at him, laying her hand on his cheek before stepping away. "Maybe I can let you go."

He felt a sliver of icy fear curl around his heart at her words.

"Come over tomorrow night. We'll talk then."

"Okay."

～

"Can William read me my bedtime story?"

Juniper looked at William in inquiry and he nodded. He was putting a very good face on it, interacting with Billy as he always did, keeping it light and fun.

As William read Billy his book, Juniper sat down on the edge of the deck that ran under the breezeway that connected the house to the shop and looked up at the sky. There was a half-moon peeking through some scattered clouds and a light dusting of stars. She drew a deep breath, marshaling all her resolve for the conversation she was about to have. She could hear William and Billy through the open bedroom window, William's voice deep and mellow, working to calm Billy's overexcited chatter. It took a little while and she let it play out, until finally she saw the light switch off. Then William was moving quietly through the door and to her side. He sat next to her on the edge of the deck.

"I can't live in Sydney."

"No."

"I wish I was stronger," she said, fervently.

He took her hand. "Don't say that."

She smiled sadly. He'd been saying that a lot lately.

"You can't live here and fulfill your commitments to your family and your business."

"No."

"What then? We live a half-life where you bounce into Blessed Inlet between location scouting missions? I sneak up to Sydney when you're in town for a dirty weekend? On those weekends when you have no parties to attend, of course, because I can't do those. And what about Billy? He loves you. He would only be confused by it all."

He nodded.

"So where does that leave us?"

He didn't answer.

"One of us has to say it, William."

"I know."

"Are you going to make it be me?"

"I don't have the strength to do it. You're stronger than me."

No, she wasn't. She felt a lump form in her throat, choking her as tears welled in her eyes. She got up and wandered away, across the yard, heard his footsteps behind her. She turned to him, gripping his shirt front in her fists. God, it hurt. So much.

He held her so tight she could barely breathe and yet she wanted him to hold her tighter still.

"I want you to do something for me."

He loosened his hold marginally. "What?"

"Do it quickly."

He took a shuddering breath, his voice tight when he said, "I can be gone tomorrow."

She quivered. That was too quick, but really, it was just torture to drag it out, so she said, "Okay." She turned in his arms and looked up at the moon.

"I won't keep the lighthouse. Any ties I keep here are only going to torture us both."

She sighed, leaning her head back against his shoulder. "Will you do one more thing for me?"

"Yes."

"Stay the night."

He blew out a breath. "Of course."

They made quiet, desperate love and held each other all night long.

∼

Juniper woke with a throbbing headache and a lump in her throat. She drew a deep, shuddering breath and pulled back to look at William. He was already awake, the look in his eyes devastating her. She reached up to brush the hair back from his forehead and he caught her hand, pressing a kiss to her palm.

"I love you," they said at the same time. Juniper smiled sadly.

They heard the patter of Billy's feet down the short hallway and Juniper saw the stricken look on William's face before he masked it, greeting her son with a cheerful smile. God, her heart hurt. Billy bounced on them both before moving to sit on William's chest, laughing. But ever sensitive, he seemed to sense the mood, because he got very quiet, and leaning down, put his hands on either side of William's face and said, "I love you."

"I love you, too," William replied huskily.

Juniper wasn't sure how much longer she could bear it. "Why don't we have breakfast?"

She let Billy have coco pops, a rare treat. They did their absolute best to keep it light and fun, but the burden of parting was too hard to bear, making their interaction stilted and false.

Juniper put the breakfast dishes in the sink, gripping the edge of the bench. She could hardly breathe. She turned to look at William, her heart squeezing painfully. He was holding Billy quietly in his lap, Billy's head resting on his shoulder. He pushed to his feet when he saw Juniper looking at him, carrying Billy outside. Juniper followed, a hot, prickly feeling overwhelming her as she stepped through the door.

"I have to go now," William said, rubbing Billy's back.

"Okay." Billy wrapped his arms around William's neck, holding on tight, as William walked down the steps.

He sat down on the edge of the deck, pulling Billy back so he could look at him, brushing his hair back from his forehead tenderly. "I can't come back anymore."

"Why?"

"Because I have to go to Sydney and look after my dad."

"But I need you to look after me."

Juniper, standing in the doorway, tried to swallow past the lump in her throat.

"Oh, mate, I wish I could. More than anything. But my dad is very sick and if I don't look after him, he'll get sicker." Juniper saw William swallow, then he said thickly, "So, I have to go. Will you do something for me?"

Billy nodded solemnly.

"Will you look after your Mum for me?"

Billy nodded again. Juniper willed the hot tears away as she walked down the steps and took Billy from William. The very least she could do was not break down in front of him. Everything that could be said between them had been said, so William just kissed Billy on his golden curls, pressed a hard kiss to Juniper's lips, then strode across the lawn and through the gate.

Mikayla, sitting at an outdoor table just down the road at Coco's, with Leah, glanced down at her phone as a message pinged. She frowned, concerned when she read it. "Oh, it's from William. Odd. It just says *Juniper needs you.* We'd better go." They gathered their bags and quickly paid for their coffee before hurrying up the street. As Mikayla stepped through the gate, she saw Juniper, sitting on the deck with Billy in her arms, frozen still. She strode over to her, stopping in her tracks as Juniper's gaze lifted to hers. The absolute desolation she saw there hit her in the guts.

"William just texted. Said you needed me?"

"He's gone." The simple words were said in such a way it was abundantly clear he wasn't coming back.

Mikayla glanced at Leah, perplexed. She'd texted the day before to ask how things had gone in Sydney, to which Juniper replied *Great. W's family is lovely.* So, she couldn't imagine what had happened between then and now to precipitate the devastation she could see on Juniper's face.

Leah stepped in, rubbing Billy's back gently. "Why don't you come with me, mate?"

Billy untangled himself from his mother, throwing himself into Leah's arms. "I want William," his voice broke and he started sobbing.

Juniper reached for him, but Leah shook her head. "I've got him," she said gently, squeezing Juniper's hand before moving away, her arms wrapped around Billy as she carried him into the house.

"What happened?" Mikayla sat down next to Juniper and put her arm around her shoulders. Juniper shook her head wordlessly. "Oh, honey, I'm sorry."

The ready sympathy broke through Juniper's control and she burst into tears, burying her face in Mikayla's shoulder and just letting go.

～

*D*ay one

Juniper woke up the next morning, feeling a heavy listlessness weighing on her. She'd let Billy sleep in her bed, taking some comfort from his warm body curled against her. He stirred, waking up and rubbing his eyes irritably. She checked the time on the bedside clock. Shit. They'd overslept. She hustled Billy out of bed, sitting him down in front of the television while she grabbed a quick shower. She had a splitting headache and that relentless weight pressing against her. She hurriedly got dressed, wrapping a towel around her head as she moved to the kitchen to get breakfast.

"Come on baby, breakfast time. You want porridge?"

"No."

She turned to look at Billy, curled up on the couch, staring at the television. "What then?"

"Nothing. Not hungry."

"You have to eat something."

"No." The belligerence in his tone was unmistakable.

"Billy," she said warningly.

He frowned at her.

"Get up to the table right now. I don't have time for this."

He dragged himself off the couch, moving to sit at the table, crossing his arms in front of him and frowning at her.

"Take that look off your face." She could hear the rising irritability in her own voice but felt powerless to stop it. Billy's scowl deepened. "If you don't tell me what you want for breakfast, you're having porridge."

As he sat there silently, frowning down at the table, she made porridge, gritting her teeth when she placed it in front of him and he pushed it away. "William," she said warningly, her heart squeezing in agony as his name rolled off her tongue.

"I'm not William! You made William go away!"

She turned away, feeling a hot rage fill her at the injustice of it. Knowing he was a darling three-year-old missing someone he loved had her wrestling with herself, trying to find the words to soothe him. She heard footsteps outside, light and female, and didn't know whether to laugh or scream when Leah opened the door and stepped inside. She took in the situation at a glance and moved to the table, grabbing the bowl of porridge. "Why don't we eat breakfast outside, hey?"

To Juniper's immense relief, Billy slid off the dining chair and allowed Leah to lead him outside.

~

*D*ay Two

Juniper woke with Billy wrapped around her, his hand resting on her cheek. She lay perfectly still, quietly breathing him in, that sticky toddler smell with a hint of the baby he'd been underlying it. He wriggled against her, lifting his head wearily. "I'm hungry."

"Are you, baby?" She brushed a hand over his curls. "What would you like for breakfast?"

"Porridge."

She carried him out to the little dining table, where he sat quietly while she made his porridge. She put the bowl down, feeling a hot lump in her throat when she saw the silent tears rolling down his cheeks. She sat down, pulling him into her lap and squeezing him tight. She didn't look up as she heard footsteps and heard Nora say, "Here now, what's this?" as she came through the door. She ran her hand over Juniper's shoulder as she moved into the kitchen to make coffee.

～

*D*ay Three
Juniper sighed with frustration and took her foot off the pedal of the pottery wheel. Unable to concentrate, she just couldn't get the balance for the bowl she was trying to throw. She gave up, moving to the sink to wash her hands. She reached for her phone, bringing up William's number, staring at it for the longest time before slipping the phone back into the pocket of her dress. She turned as she heard the back door of the workroom open and Mikayla step through, a bottle of wine in her hand. "Come on, love. Let's get pissed."

～

*D*ay Six
Juniper woke alone, the pale fingers of a cold sunrise creeping across the floor and up onto her bed. It was the first night Billy had slept the whole night through in his own bed since William had left. She went to check on him. Sound asleep. She couldn't go back to bed, so she grabbed her dressing gown and making a coffee, went out to sit on the deck, rubbing her chest as the ever-present band tightened around her heart. She

almost smiled as Rafe came through the gate and moved across the yard to sit down next to her.

"What are you doing here this early?"

"Just got off shift. Thought I'd check on you."

He put his arm around her, and she let go, crying into his shoulder.

~

*D*ay Ten

Friday. The end of an impossibly long week. Juniper lay in bed, staring at the ceiling, trying to force herself to get up. Then she frowned. Billy was up. She could hear Bluey playing on the television. She sighed, sliding out of bed and into her robe. She stopped dead at the loungeroom door. John, sitting on the couch with Billy curled up next to him, turned his head. "Coffee's on," he said, gesturing to the kitchen.

~

*D*ay Eleven

"What is this, 'The Everybody Make Sure Juniper Doesn't Fall to Pieces Brigade'?" She didn't even try to hide the irritation in her voice as she cleared the breakfast dishes off the table.

"Something like that," Callum replied calmly from the lounge-room, helping Billy put his sandals on.

She was fed up. Sick of being checked up on, sick of being sympathized with. Sick of pretending she was getting better. She was just fucking sick of everything. She told him so.

"Stop pretending then. You aren't fooling anyone anyway," he said bluntly.

They stared at each other, then something about the situation tickled her sense of humor. Her lips quirked in a rare smile. "I'm sorry."

He smiled back. "Don't worry about it.

He came over to her, looking down at her for a long moment, his hazel eyes intense. Something she saw there resonated with her. He knew exactly how she was feeling. He surprised her by pressing a kiss to her forehead before saying, "You'll be alright."

"Will I?"

"Yes. I promise." There was a sort of comfort to be had in the simple sincerity of the statement. The fact that he seemed to believe it meant maybe she could, too. "We're going to the beach and then the ice cream shop. We'll be back in about an hour."

"Okay."

~

*D*ay Fourteen

Juniper smiled as she watched Leah chase Billy across the beach. "She's been an absolute blessing."

"She's a gem," Mikayla agreed.

Sighing, Juniper continued on, the sea pulling gently at her feet as she walked along the water's edge, the light sea breeze softly caressing her skin. Mikayla had also been a blessing. She was pretty sure it was Mikayla coordinating the constant check ins and support. "You're such a good friend to me." She felt that ever present lump thicken in her throat.

Mikayla slipped her arm through Juniper's, pulling her along. "I hate seeing you like this."

"I hate being like this." They walked on for a little longer in silence. "When is it going to get easier?"

"I don't know, darling. It's only been a few weeks. Give yourself time. Although..."

Juniper filled in the blanks in her mind. *Although, you're pretty devastated and broken, so you know, maybe never. Maybe it's just never going to get easier.* She took a deep breath. "You know, it would be easier if he didn't love me. It hurts more knowing that he hurts, too."

"I know," Mikayla said quietly. "There's just nothing you could do?"

Juniper shook her head. "I don't think so. There are just so many layers to it. His family needs him. It would devastate his father if they had to lose the business. They can't keep the business without William. So, could he live here and run the business? No, not without traveling to Sydney every other day for business meetings and whatever else he does. Those hideous business functions." She shivered at the memory. "Could I live in Sydney? No."

"Are you sure? Could you live in Sydney and just not attend the hideous business functions?"

"I really thought about that and if it was only the business functions that were the problem, then maybe I could. But it's not only the horrid parties, is it? It's the whole package. I mean, what school would Billy go to? What kind of people would we be associating with every day? Could you imagine him at kindergarten, telling someone he can see their colors?"

"Shit."

"Yeah, shit."

"So, that's it then? He's never coming back?"

Juniper felt the weight of it pressing on her chest. "No, he's never coming back."

～

*L*ife in Sydney was really just a matter of going through the motions; business meetings, another stupid party, traveling interstate to inspect a property, family dinners. His family had been utterly shocked when he'd come from that last, agonizing trip to Blessed Inlet and, calling an emergency meeting, said they had to sell the lighthouse. Cassie immediately bombarded him with questions. It took every ounce of control he had not to scream at her, so he turned away, moving over to the window and staring out wordlessly.

"Don't tell me to shush, Mum! Look at him!"

"I'm fine, Cassie."

"The fuck you are!"

He ground his teeth, his hands balled into fists in his pockets. He was so very far from fine but since the only solution was betraying them all and running away, he just had to stick it out. Just keep breathing in and out until it got easier. In the end, they acquiesced on his request to sell the lighthouse and that's all he needed so he left the meeting.

On impulse, he ordered some blocks of wood online, in varying sizes and types; walnut, balsa wood, oak, cherry. He'd made Billy's frog pond out of balsa wood. It was good but too soft, not providing enough of a challenge for what he had in mind. The cherry was almost unworkable since he was so out of practice. He'd had to order new tools because he'd blunted the blades on the original set and he just couldn't get the flow with it. He decided he liked the walnut best; once he'd experimented with a mallet in conjunction with the carving tool it seemed to work.

He set it up on the dining room table in his suite, spending every available moment on it, until it fast became an obsession. It was ten o'clock at night and there he was, leaning over the table, working away. He was oblivious to the spectacular view out of his wide windows, the bridge standing sentinel over the always moving ships across the water. He'd forgotten to eat dinner. That was becoming a bad habit.

The elevator bell rang. Frowning in frustration at the interruption, he glanced up. His mother stepped into the living area, a covered tray in her hands.

"I stopped at the kitchen before coming up. They said you hadn't ordered dinner."

He shrugged. "I wasn't hungry."

"Well, you need to eat, regardless. They had some ravioli left so I've brought that for you."

"Thanks."

He heard Gwen move across the room, but kept his gaze averted, concentrating on pushing the carving knife carefully into the wood, shaving off a curl of walnut and letting it fall to the table. She stood next to him, watching him work for a long moment, before pushing aside the tools he had laid out on the table and dunking the tray in front of him, lifted the lid. He glanced up at her, ready with an angry protest.

"You're about ten seconds away from an intervention, son. Eat." Only to mollify her, he picked up the knife and fork and removed the serviette, taking a bite of ravioli while she watched him. Satisfied when he put a second forkful in his mouth, she ran her hand affectionately across his shoulder before going to the minibar and getting them a beer each. Handing him his, she took a sip, leaning a hip on the table edge, picking up some wood shavings in her hand. "Walnut. An interesting choice."

"It's got the right finish."

"I see." She let the shavings drop back to the table. "I want you to tell me what's going on."

"Nothing. I'm carving wood and eating ravioli." He took another bite, looking at her with a challenge in his eye.

She sighed, reaching out to push his hair back from his forehead tenderly. "You decided you didn't love her?"

He flinched.

"Oh. She decided she didn't love you."

He dropped the fork. It landed on the plate with a loud clatter.

"So, you love each other. What, then?"

Fuck, she was persistent. "She can't live in Sydney."

"That I can understand. But what about you?"

He looked up at her then, for a long time. He watched as comprehension flashed in her eyes. "You've sacrificed yourself, your happiness, for us?"

"For Dad."

She pressed her fingers to her lips, struggling for control. "Oh, darling. Your father would be devastated if he knew."

"I know. That's why I haven't told you." He pushed the plate away and reached for the bottle of beer. "But don't you think it would be worse if I left? You've said it yourself, Mum. It would kill him. The only thing keeping him going is this business and let's be real, you can't run it without me."

She looked away, gazing out the window unseeingly for a long moment. "I wish you'd spoken to me about this."

He shrugged. "It's for the best. Juniper understands." God, it hurt his heart just to say her name. "She'll move on, meet someone else and I'll..." He couldn't finish the sentence.

Gwen pushed up from the table, saying, "You know best, I suppose." She leaned down and pressed a kiss to his forehead. "I love you."

He picked up a chisel, leaning forward and delicately scraping it across the wood. "I love you, too," he said without looking. She took it for the dismissal it was and walked out.

CHAPTER 10

*D*ay Twenty-Nine

Juniper moved around the yard listlessly, stringing paper party streamers from the deck to the oak tree. If she were honest, she'd never felt less like celebrating her birthday. She'd been inclined to just give it a miss, but Mikayla was absolutely insistent. Since she'd roped Billy into the plans, there was really no avoiding it. He was having a hard enough time coping since William had left, anything she could do to make him feel better, she would do.

Mikayla bounced out of the house. "Billy's not happy with your present. He wants to get you something else. Alright if I take him down the street?"

Juniper sighed. "Sure. That's lovely. Thank you."

Mikayla came over and took the streamer from Juniper, reaching up with her extra height and winding it around a branch. "Bit of a shit birthday, hey."

"Yeah, a bit."

Mikayla gave her arm a sympathetic rub. "I wish it hadn't turned out that way."

"Me too. Right now, I wish I could get to feeling better about it all."

"It's only been a month."

"True."

A subdued Billy came out of the house with his sandals on and walked down the steps. "I'm ready, Mikky."

Juniper sighed again as Mikayla and Billy left. It wasn't getting better. She wasn't getting better. The pain was as sharp now as it had been on the day William had left. She wondered if they'd made a mistake, been too hasty. Could there be a compromise to be had somewhere that would give her a little bit of happiness? She wondered whether they had really explored all the options. They'd never allowed themselves to talk about the future in any depth, before they'd recognized that they didn't have one. Her thoughts traveled down a very worn track. The first stop - the ultimate fantasy of William somehow living in Blessed Inlet. The second stop – some half-life where they snatched visits where they could. The third stop – her moving to Sydney. Seeing as there was no way William could leave his family in the lurch, and a half measure would almost be worse than nothing, that left the third option. Maybe she could see a therapist. Or maybe there was some drug she could take. Anti-anxiety medication was a thing. She felt her heartbeat fluttering uncomfortably at her throat at the very idea. She drifted over to the box of paper decorations she'd made with Billy, pressing her hand to her heart, trying to alleviate the ache. She was dimly aware of the sound of a car pulling up out the front and a frown of annoyance creased her brows. She'd shut the shop for her birthday, and she really didn't feel up to explaining to some demanding customer why she couldn't serve them today. Maybe it would be easier just to serve them. Then knowing her luck, they'd want to browse, or ask ridiculous questions. She heard a car door open and close, then silence as she waited for the sound of the knock at the shop door.

She felt the hairs on the back of her neck prickle, and she turned to the gate. Her heart squeezed painfully as she gasped and let the streamers drop from her nerveless fingers. "William," she whispered. She watched him move towards her as though in a dream until he was standing in front of her, his eyes alight as they roved over her face.

"Hey."

Her lips moved, but no sound came out. She just stood there staring at him. He reached out and stroked a finger lightly down her cheek and she blinked as her eyes blurred with tears.

"It's your birthday."

She nodded.

"I made you something." He held out a gift-wrapped box, smiling at her with such tenderness she felt a little sliver of nervous hope sneak into her heart.

She took it from him and sat on the edge of the deck, staring at him as he moved to sit beside her. She couldn't stop staring at him, drinking him in hungrily. Still smiling, he gestured at the box. "Open it."

She dragged her eyes away from his beautiful face and, looking down at the gift, weighed it experimentally in her hands. Heavy. Solid. With shaking fingers, she peeled back the wrapping paper and, scrunching it up, dropped it next to her. Then she laid the box in her lap and seeing a tab along the edge, ran her finger under it and lifted it.

"Ooooh," she gasped, raising brimming eyes to his face. "Oh, god. It's beautiful." She looked down at the box in her lap, running a finger gently over the exquisitely carved statue, reaching under to lift it from the box. Tears sliding down her face she gazed at it in wonder. It was her, holding Billy in her arms, his head resting on her shoulder. He had one arm around her neck, his other hand resting on her cheek. Her feet wear bare. It was so exquisitely carved you could almost imagine the skirt of her dress moving in the breeze. Her eyes were closed, and a gentle smile curved her lips.

"Happy birthday."

"Thank you," she said, turning to look at him. She wanted desperately to reach out and touch him but felt unsure. If this was a flying visit to acknowledge her birthday, she wasn't sure how to respond. It was sweet and wonderful, of course, but also heart breaking. There would be no way she could let Billy see him if he was here just for the day; it would confuse and upset him too much. But there was that look in his eyes, the way he was watching her. Cradling the statue close, she wiped her hand across her cheeks.

"What are you doing here, William?"

"Well, now, there's a story." He took her hand, linking his fingers through hers. She let him, because it felt so lovely, and she'd been craving it. "I've been a bit of a mess, Juniper."

"Me too," she said quietly, causing him to tighten his hold on her fingers.

"I thought I was doing a pretty good job of hiding it, but apparently not. I hadn't told anyone what happened between us, I just said it didn't work out. One night, Mum came over. She saw what I was making." He gestured to the figurine in her arms. "It wasn't your gift, at that stage, because I didn't think I was going to see you again. It was for me." He let out a shuddering breath and she shifted a little closer, watching his face intently. "Of course, she knew straight away that I was still in love with you, so then she asked me if the problem was you." He reached up and tucked a curl behind her ear. "I got a bit defensive, so that gave the game away. She figured out pretty quickly what had happened, but she just left me to it." He smiled at her. "Behind my back, however, she called a family meeting. A whole lot of action happened that is too boring to go into right now, but the end result might interest you."

Juniper let out a breath she hadn't been aware of holding. "What was the end result?"

"They fired me."

She gasped. "William! No!"

His smile widened, the glow in his eyes shooting straight through her. "Yes."

"Are you okay with it?" She reached a tentative hand up to touch his face and he turned his head, pressing his lips to her palm.

"I wasn't, at first. I was so torn." He closed the space between them and wrapped his arm around her waist, taking the figurine from her and placing it gently on the deck. "I was so afraid I was being selfish and letting them down. But they had it all arranged. I'll tell you all the nitty gritty details later. But for now, I want you to know that I love you desperately and I want to stay here. With you."

With the emotion swirling inside her finally erupting, Juniper burst into tears. She wrapped her arms around his neck as he pulled her tight against him, burying his face in her hair and holding her while she cried, letting go of all the agony of the past weeks. When she was done, she raised her head to look at him and, brushing his hair back from his forehead, took his face in her hands and pressed a gentle kiss to his lips. "I love you."

"I love you, too." Then he kissed her, and went on kissing her as the autumn sunshine spilled over them. He finally lifted his head to look at her. "I love you,"

She gave a sighing laugh. "I love you, too."

"William!"

Juniper's breath caught in her throat at the look of utter joy in William's eyes before he turned to look at Billy, racing down the drive. William jumped to his feet, taking three big strides across the lawn as Billy ran to him, squealing with delight as William swept him up in his arms and spun him around before pulling him in for a fierce hug. Juniper's heart nearly burst with happiness as she watched them. Billy's arms and legs were wrapped around William, squeezing him with every muscle in his little body. William, his eyes closed, his hand cradling the back of Billy's head.

"I missed you."

"I missed you, too." William carried Billy back to the deck and sat down next to Juniper.

Just then, Mikayla called from the gate, "Hey, lovebirds!"

Juniper looked over.

Mikayla was grinning from ear to ear, her eyes glistening. "Party still on?"

"You bet!"

She gave a wave. "I'll come back later then."

Juniper turned back to Billy, reaching out to ruffle his blonde curls as he rested his head on William's shoulder. "What do you reckon? Pretty good to see William?"

He nodded. "But I'll miss him when he goes," he said sadly.

"Well, guess what?"

"What?" Billy asked, lifting his head and looking at William.

"I'm not going."

Billy tilted his head to one side inquiringly. "Ever?"

"That's right. I'm going to stay here. With you."

"In my house?" Billy asked excitedly.

"Well, that's something I have to talk to your Mum about." William turned to Juniper. "You've got time to go for a drive?"

Very curious, Juniper nodded. "Sure." She dashed inside to grab her bag and put the figurine on the table, coming out and taking William's hand as he carried Billy out of the yard. She stopped dead at the end of her drive when she saw where he was headed. "You got a new car?"

He was standing next to a blue Mercedes GLS. He grinned as he opened the back passenger door and helped Billy into a booster seat.

"With a kid's seat?" She came up next to him.

"Yep. How else would I drive my family around? You all good there, mate?"

Billy nodded enthusiastically.

"Definitely no going back, then?"

"Definitely no going back." He closed the door and pressed a quick kiss to her lips before opening the door for her.

She sighed blissfully, sliding into the car and putting her seat belt on. More than curious, she watched as he drove, glancing at him as he turned onto the gravel road that led up to the lighthouse.

He parked out the front of the long building and looking through the windscreen at it for a long moment, nodded with satisfaction.

"You didn't put it on the market?"

"No, I couldn't quite push myself to do it." They piled out of the car, Billy immediately holding his arms up for William to carry him. She watched for a moment as he crunched across the gravel, her son's arm tight around his neck, her heart soaring. He stopped and turned, holding out his hand. "You coming?"

She moved to him, linking her fingers through his, pleased but also a little confused. He led her to the long house, taking a key from his pocket and opening the main door. She'd only looked inside once, when he'd brought her here on their first date. He'd explained how perfect it would be as a corporate retreat and she could see what he meant. "Look around and tell me what you think." She stepped through the door and looked around.

"You don't mean for us to live here?" The confusion was evident in her tone as she wandered into the middle of the room, gazing around.

"Not us, no. This would be the artist's studio and accommodation."

"Artists?" She spun around to look at him.

He was grinning now, enjoying himself hugely.

She looked around again, really able to see what he was talking about. "An Artist's colony," she all but whispered.

"Yes. So, this building for a studio and accommodation and the stables could be for exhibitions and functions if we wanted. Or not. Whatever." He shrugged.

She felt goosebumps on her arms. "It's perfect."

"You like it?"

She walked over to him, sliding her arm around his waist and resting her head on his shoulder. "I love it. I absolutely love it."

He kissed the top of her head. "I was thinking the little cottage could be used for our own family when they visit, and we can live in the big house. It needs a bit of work, so we'd have to stay in the cottage in the meantime, or I stay with you. Or we don't do any of it and I learn how to make pottery."

She laughed. "Let's do it."

"I'll buy a pottery wheel then."

She laughed again. "No, let's do this." She waved her arm in a sweeping gesture around the room.

She felt him take a deep, shuddering breath and she lifted her head to look at him, her heart slayed by the glow in his eyes. "God, I love you."

"I love you, too." He pulled her tight against him.

"I love you!"

"I love you, too, you little scoundrel."

They laughed at Billy's giggle as they walked back out into the warm sunshine and he squirmed to get down, skipping across the grass. "I have to show you one more thing before we head back for your birthday party."

"Okay."

He led them across the lawn to the lighthouse and up the stairs. They stood at the wide windows, looking out over the bright blue of the Tasman Sea.

"Juniper."

She looked over at him and something in his eyes stopped her breath.

"I have some things I want to say."

"Alright."

His tone had caught Billy's attention. Sensing something important, he'd reached up for Juniper to pick him up, gazing at William quietly. She forced herself to take a deep breath as her heart started hammering in her chest.

He stood before her, his hands in the pockets of his jeans, balled into fists. "Before I met you and Billy, I was heading down a well-planned road. I should have been happy. But I wasn't. I was restless and frustrated and I didn't know why." He reached out and stroked Billy's hair tenderly. "Then you came along, and everything changed. I felt at peace. Happy. You've given me —" He paused, swallowing, his voice thick when he resumed. "Juniper, you've given me a chance at a better life than I ever imagined for myself." He pulled his hand out of his pocket and she looked down, her heart thudding faster than ever. He held a ring box in plush, maroon velvet. "Will you give me the chance to make you as happy as you've made me? Will you let me be a dad to Billy? Will you marry me?" He opened the box and she gasped, holding her hand over her heart, tears rolling down her cheeks. Nestled in the box was a ring with a shimmering, milky moonstone, flanked by diamonds.

She couldn't speak past the lump in her throat, so she nodded, wrapping her free arm around his neck, pulling him tight against her. Billy shifted his weight and William caught him, holding them both. She kissed him, taking a half step away as he juggled the ring box and Billy. Laughing breathlessly, she took it from him and slid the ring on her finger, spreading her fingers out to admire it as it shimmered in the sunlight.

"So, that's a yes, then?"

"Yes! Absolutely yes!" She gazed at him, all the love she felt for him filling her up.

At that moment, Billy placed his hands on William's cheeks and turned him so they were looking at each other and said, "*Now* can I call you Daddy?" As if he'd been waiting an eternity to do so.

Fresh tears spilled over as William looked at her for permission and she nodded wordlessly.

"Yes, you sure can," he said thickly.

Her heart so full she thought it would burst, Juniper kissed them both then said, "We'd better get back. I think the party's already started."

Billy squirmed to get down as they stepped onto the lawn. "Daddy! Check this out! I can do a somersault."

William pulled Juniper against him as they watched Billy's attempt at a somersault. "Wow, that's amazing!" He said enthusiastically. "It's all amazing," he said softly, turning to Juniper and pressing a lingering kiss to her lips. "I love you."

Her smile radiant, she replied, "I love you, too."

He took her hand and walked to the car, calling for Billy to come. As he helped the little boy into his seat and did the belt up, he wondered how long it would take for the buzz to wear off. Here he was, with the woman of his dreams and her beautiful child – his family. He got in the front seat and pressed the start button, glancing over at Juniper. She was still smiling at him with that sense of wonder that pulled at his heart because he felt the exact same way.

"Tell me what happened in Sydney," she said as he turned the car around and headed down the gravel road.

"Well, as I said, Mum saw how I was, guessed what was behind it, and sprang into action. By the time they told me about it, it was a done deal. Cassie's fiancée, James, is going to step into my role. Things haven't been right at his company for a long while, so he was already looking for a change. We know he can do the work as it's not too different from what he's done before. I'll be responsible for development planning – budgeting for property purchases and renovations, meeting with Cassie on a monthly basis to discuss the performance of existing properties. It's what Dad does, mostly, so I'll be there as backup. I'll be able to do most of it via video link. Other than that, my main role is developing Locke Industries' first ever artist's colony." It still amazed him how neatly it had all fallen into place.

"Are you sure it's all okay?"

He smiled at her. "I'm sure. Once Dad said that the business was meant to be their legacy to me and Cassie, not a prison, that cemented it for me, because it had started to feel exactly like a prison." He pulled the car to the curb in front of the shop, pausing to look at her again, just to bask in the wonder of being with her. "Let's go celebrate your birthday."

As they walked through the gate at the top of the drive, it was obvious that Mikayla had told everyone he was back, as they weren't at all surprised to see him. They weren't surprised, but they were definitely pleased. Mikayla threw herself at him as he walked down the drive, wrapping her arms around his neck and squeezing tight. "Welcome home," she said quietly.

"Thank you."

She kissed his cheek before moving aside so that Nora could step in and give him an exuberant hug. After that, it was back slaps and handshakes from John, Callum and Rafe, then Leah stepped up, surprising him with a shy kiss on the cheek, saying softly, "We missed you," quickly stepping away before he had a chance to reply. He sat down next to Juniper on the long bench, in the shade of the old oak tree, watching as she slowly, deliberately, brushed her hair off her forehead with her left hand. She laughed uproariously as Mikayla squealed at the sight of the engagement ring, skipping over to grab Juniper's hand and examine the ring minutely. William glanced around, catching sight of Rafe, watching Mikayla with a look of such raw longing on his face that William hastily looked away.

"Wow, you sure move fast!" Mikayla said after everyone had offered hugs and congratulations.

William grinned at her. "Why wait?"

"Oooh, quick wedding then?"

They both looked at Juniper, William feeling his heart soar at her enthusiastic nod. He leaned back, putting his arm around Juniper's shoulders, looking out over the yard, observing everyone as they mingled, still amazed that this much happiness was possible.

From not wanting to celebrate her birthday at all, Juniper now wanted it to go forever, so once they'd finished their food and sat around for a while, she got to her feet. "I want to go for a walk," she announced.

"Excellent idea." Mikayla, ever active, bounced to her feet and headed up the drive. "Let's go to the beach. I'll grab a footy from the car."

"I'm not kicking the footy," Juniper stated, following her.

"Spoil sport. Rafe'll kick with me."

"Of course," Rafe replied, throwing Billy up on his shoulders as they headed down the footpath.

Juniper fell into step beside William, linking her fingers with his. He surprised her when he tugged on her hand, slowing them down so that the rest of the group ambled ahead. "What do you think about Rafe and Mikayla?"

"In what way?" She asked with a confused frown.

"In a getting together kind of way."

She watched them for a long moment, walking by all the shop fronts, Mikayla chatting animatedly while Rafe bent his head in her direction to listen. He laughed at something she'd said and she grinned up at him impishly. "I'm not sure, to be honest. There's energy between them. They have a beautiful friendship, but...I don't know. People keep assuming they're in a relationship, but they keep insisting that they're just friends."

"Right."

They reached the beach and the group spread out to play kick to kick, in the soft light of the setting sun. After standing around watching for a little while, Juniper slipped her sandals off and wandered away to walk along the shoreline. She smiled as William joined her, putting his arm around her shoulders. The din from the football game faded away as they walked, the sound of the waves lapping gently at the hem of Juniper's dress the only sound. She came to a stop, turning into William, resting her head on his shoulder, smiling when he kissed the top of her head. Such a beautiful sense of peace and wellbeing washed through her, healing all the agony of the previous weeks.

"You know what?"

"What?" She asked, lifting her head to look at him.

"The best things in life really are free."

She sighed happily. "They sure are. I love you."

"I love you, too."

THANK YOU!

If you're not ready to leave Blessed Inlet, here's a cheeky preorder link for Mikayla and Rafe:

My Book

For bonus scenes and exclusive content, you can subscribe to the Mary Waterford newsletter here:

https://www.marywaterford.com/

ABOUT THE AUTHOR

WHO ARE WE?

We're two sisters, Susan and Kate, who live on opposite sides of the world and decided after a year of closed borders to write romance novels together!

Australian born and bred, Kate moved to Germany in 2001 and has been there ever since. Between us, we have five children and three dogs and we've always shared a love of reading, passed down to us through our mother and grandparents. Our pseudonym, Mary Waterford, honors our maternal grandmother (one of her favorite authors was Maeve Binchy!)

We both believe that reading - regardless of the genre - offers an escape from real life; whether it's chasing criminals with Eve Dallas or fighting off Voldemort with Harry Potter or riding in a carriage through Regency London with Mr. Beaumaris, reading is more important now, in these crazy times, than ever.

Our goal is to offer our readers that same escape, with relatable, loveable characters and locations that take you out of the lounge room and into the quiet sleepy beach town of Blessed Inlet, or into the hustle and bustle of New York City.

Printed in Great Britain
by Amazon